Book Two of the Endless Breath Saga

A Scream
Through Time

Nicholas Licalsi

STEP INTO THE ROAD

For my brother Andrew, you push me to want better in my self and my world!

Thank You Patrons!

Thank You Patrons!

There's nothing quite like the magic of exploring new worlds and
meeting unique characters through storytelling.
And there's *absolutely* nothing like the magic of knowing that there
are people willing to support that expedition.
This story is my bounty. I hope you enjoy it.

Katelyn Combs, Bonnie Adams, BW, Melinda Callender,
Roy & Beth Shockey, Sam Meeks, John Middleton, Matt VanNatten.

Join the crew at: https://patreon.com/stepintotheroad

This book discusses suicide and suicidal idealization.

If you are in emotional distress or suicidal crisis, you are not alone. Call the US National Suicide Prevention Lifeline at 988 to speak with a trained counselor. It's free, confidential, and available 24/7.

For my readers outside the United States you can find a hotline for your area here:
https://en.wikipedia.org/wiki/List_of_suicide_crisis_lines

1

Gretchen stood in front of me on the roof of her apartment building, precariously balanced on the half wall that ran around the perimeter. The building was downtown, although which town I never learned. Cars passed by the building but they did not honk incessantly so I knew it wasn't a major metroplex.

I'd followed Gretchen here, not by walking behind her on the flight of stairs, but through time and space. Her bloodcurdling scream called my name, I heard it as soon as I left the younger version of myself and a parallel version of her, to enjoy their coffee at the Light House Café.

The apartment roof was unfinished, designed for maintenance workers to access equipment, not for residents to come and relax. The tension in Gretchen's shoulders and dark bags under her eyes indicated she hadn't relaxed in a long time. She was close enough to the ledge that she wouldn't relax if she valued her life.

Capped metal vents were clustered around the roof like mushrooms. Air conditioners hummed, fighting back the heat of the summer sun. The fire escape door squeaked on rusty hinges as it blew in the breeze. Gretchen hadn't cared to close it behind her.

The breeze carried gray storm clouds towards us from the horizon. Anything lower than clouds was blocked by a wall of skyscrapers. This apartment was far from the tallest building around. But it was high enough to suit Gretchen's needs.

Gretchen smelled different from the younger version I'd killed countless times. Her perfume carried hints of orange and lemon instead of cherry blossoms. It was only a perceptible change because I'd spent so much time around her recently.

I tasted sweat in my mouth. My long brown leather coat was not suited for the day's heat. It rippled in the breeze, but the wind did little to cool me.

Gretchen wore a sun dress. She wasn't in high school anymore, probably about to graduate college by my best guess. She wore sandals and next to her feet sat a small clutch purse with a bright pink paisley pattern. Her blond hair whipped around her face masking her terrified eyes.

"Get away from me, Todd!" she shouted.

I wondered how she knew who I was. I wore a scruffy face much older than the high school version she knew. But that was a question for another time and place.

I raised my hands in surrender. I wasn't going to hurt her today, I was done with that. "Let's step down from there," I said and offered my hand to help.

She flinched at my movement and teetered on the lip of the wall. Someone shouted from below.

"It's okay," I assured her. "You don't want to do this."

"You're going to kill me." Gretchen sobbed in terror. Her tears caught her hair which slowly quit flapping in the wind. "I've seen you do it!"

"I'm not going to hurt you," I assured her. It was true but I felt like a wolf speaking to a sheep. "Where did you see me before?"

"In my dreams. Every night I watch you kill me. I haven't slept for days."

Dreams, I hadn't had them in ages. I hadn't slept in ages either. Gretchen was tired, people acted silly when they were tired. "They're just dreams. They can't hurt you." Assessing the situation I doubted Gretchen was in my grasp. I could lunge to catch her, but it wasn't a guarantee.

"Every night, I watch you choose just the right brownie on the assembly line and place a deadly peanut in the batter. I feel my throat constrict and I wake up gasping looking for my EpiPen."

She was right, that was one of my preferred ways to kill her in order to get the attention of my younger self. However, this Gretchen, the one that belonged to the timeline we stood in, shouldn't remember that. It happened far away in one of the infinite universes that I traveled through. I could kill thousands of Gretchen, likely did, and it'd be a drop in the barrel of infinity.

"I had to do it," I said. "I'm done now though."

"It's still happening." Gretchen gestured at the world around us between her sobs. "It's not over. It will never be over."

"It is over. They're just dreams, " I assured her. She didn't look like she believed me, so I decided to lie. "You have an exciting life ahead of you! Full of meaningful memories you'll make with others. Friends, family, maybe kids. They don't want you to do this right now." In truth the universe was indifferent to her, it was indifferent to me and I could travel through it.

"I'll never sleep again. I can't do it." She looked over her shoulder to measure something in her gymnast mind, assuming she did gymnastics in this universe.

I took advantage of the pause and lurched towards her to pull her off the wall. Gretchen turned back, her ears must've alerted her to my movement. She scampered back. Maybe she forgot she was on the ledge. Maybe she thought what lay below was less terrifying than me.

She fell backwards. My hand passed over her thin dress but didn't grip anything. She tucked her arms and head in reflexively. While it would've helped her when landing on a padded gym floor it'd do little for her now.

I leaned over the ledge. My hand nearly knocked her purse off. I clutched it to save it from the fate of falling. I was infinitely more successful at rescuing it.

The crowd gathered below parted like rippling water. Gretchen landed and the crowd let out a unified scream.

I turned back from the ledge, Gretchen's purse still in my hand. I started my focused breathing. It was time to leave this universe. There were infinitely more interesting places than this. I could go be a captain on a Star Liner cruise starship again. Those trips through the cosmos were always fun.

Sirens sounded around the corner. Someone would be investigating her death. They wouldn't get far. It'd likely be chalked up to another suicide due to the stress of college.

That was all it was. She was sleep-deprived, not thinking straight. But how had I heard her scream? How did she know who I was? I quit breathing like I was going to leave. I went to the stairs and looked through her purse on the way down.

It wasn't a big purse. It had some cash, a few plastic cards, a makeup kit, small pen, notebook, and flip phone. I played with the old-style phone and wondered why it wasn't more advanced. It was blue and shaped like a river rock. It had an enamel pug looped as a trinket around the stubby antenna.

Maybe she was short on money. I'd bought burner phones like this in various universes. But with the amount of cash in her wallet that seemed unlikely. What college kid carried around this much money? I had a few unsavory ideas but none of them suited Gretchen as I knew her.

I stepped out of the stairwell and walked through the lobby of the apartment complex. I tried to remember my college experience. My home universe, my original life, it was so far back in my past I didn't remember it. But I could remember more recent lives I'd lived, like the one I lived with Gretchen after saving her from being run over. In that one, my phone had a touch screens and apps to transfer money digitally.

The sun shone in my eyes as I walked out of the apartment lobby. A few people in the crowd looked at me. Police were interviewing others. I turned away from the crowd and walked down the street. It felt strange holding a bright pink purse with my long coat so I stuffed it in the large inside pocket of my jacket.

***

After putting some distance between me and the crowd I smelled buttery baked goods and easily found the source. A small bakery had its door propped open with a foldable slate sidewalk sign. Someone had doodled the day's specials on it with chalk, but I had no doubt that the smell was doing far more marketing for the place.

I stood in line. Most of the customers seemed to be college-age. Groups studied sharing textbooks and notes. Strangely, no one had a laptop out. A man in a suit talked loudly on a phone in the corner. His phone also flipped open, despite his suit indicating he could afford something much nicer if it existed.

"What can I get you?" The young man at the cash register asked me.

"Lemon poppy seed muffin." I gestured to the row of them sitting in the display case.

"Anything to drink?" He asked while punching my order in on a plastic keyboard.

"Coffee," I replied, "Lots of cream and sugar."

"Cream and sugar is over there," the cashier pointed at a small kiosk near the man on the phone. He read off my total, it wasn't as much as I expected.

I pulled some cash out of Gretchen's wallet. Was it stealing if she was dead?

The young man gave me a funny look as I pulled the money out of the purse, but he didn't say anything.

"I thought it matched my eyes nicely." I held the purse up to my face to give him the opportunity to judge.

He let out a forced laugh. Humor was always tough to transfer across the multiverse. I passed him the cash and he gave me my change followed by my food and drink.

After filling my coffee to the brim with cream and sugar I found a small table away from the door. With my back to the wall, I shrugged off my jacket. I picked off pieces from the muffin top and flipped through the plastic cards in Gretchen's wallet. She only had one debit and one credit card, the rest were gift cards, memberships, and various ID cards for school and driving. They sat in front of me like I was playing poker with friends. Much like cards in poker, they gave me little to work with.

I pulled out the notebook hoping it'd be more interesting. The cover matched the pink paisley purse and a small magnetic clasp held it shut. The first few pages were marked up with to-do lists filled with homework and chores. Gretchen's handwriting was soft and curved as I remembered.

As I flipped through, the dates at the top of the page jumped a few years and the handwriting became difficult to read. Occasionally a familiar curved "c" or "n" popped up but the majority of the print was jagged and unevenly spaced letters as if a songbird once walked across the pages.

Doing my best to read the handwriting I found it was a story. Unfortunately, it wasn't a very good story. It was littered with amateurish "and thens," it jumped locations without explanation, and each scene failed to come together in a meaningful conclusion. After a few pages, it ended with "...and then I woke up." I realized it was a dream journal.

I put the clasp over the page I'd read to hold my place, hoping I wouldn't have to go back to it. Reading someone else's dreams was not the way I wanted to spend my time in this, or any, universe. I flipped the phone open, the enamel pug trinket knocked against my knuckle. I started to search for my name in her contacts.

The problem with traveling the multiverse is that technology is never consistent. Keyboard layouts change frequently and this phone was no exception. The key for 0 sat in the top right corner of the number pad with each sequential number below it. There were only two columns of numbers which left space for shortcut keys on the sides. My thumb cramped while I tried to select the right letters, which were assigned chaotically to each number key. It was like some universes tried their hardest to find the least optimal solution.

I finally input my name to the search bar of the contacts screen but nothing came up for Todd or Rungson. It might be under a nickname so I tried remembering my recent high school phone number, on the unlikely chance it was the same.

"Sir," a woman's voice said to me. "Is this stuff yours?"

"Of course. It's at my table isn't it?" I didn't appreciate the interruption. I was trying to remember if the fifth digit in my old phone number was a 6 or a 9. I popped the last of the muffin into my mouth, while I chewed on my memory.

I could feel the lady looming over me. Without swallowing I asked, "Do you have a problem with my fashion choices?"

"I do." She didn't hide that she was in less of a mood for a joke than the cashier.

I looked up and realized why. She wore a dark navy blue collared shirt with patches on each shoulder. The tool belt around her waist was filled with all kinds of gadgets most notably a bright yellow gun on her right hip. Her partner, a young man, wore a matching uniform. They had matching shiny silver police badges pinned to their chest.

The only thing that didn't match were their name tags. Atkinson was pinned to her chest while her partner wore a name with far too many consonants and not enough vowels.

That was faster than expected, I thought. "Maybe you're just jealous because you have to wear such a dull uniform." I smiled at her then licked my teeth to make sure they were clean, glad I'd taken the chance to finish the muffin. In my haste a poppy seed had lodged itself near my right canine tooth so I picked at it with my pinky finger.

The entire bakery stared at us. Even the suit on the phone had decided to talk at a reasonable level while he stole glances over at us.

I considered putting on a show for the place. No handcuffs or jail cells could hold me. And even if I was able to be killed, nothing on their belt was lethal.

I didn't know my rights, laws change from universe to universe, so that put me at a disadvantage. But it hardly felt like a fair handicap.

"Then you are," the police officer turned Gretchen's ID so she could read it. "Gretchen Smith?"

Was Gretchen's last name really Smith? No wonder I had a hard time remembering it.

"Not much of a resemblance," the young partner tacked on. Officer Atkinson wiped the smile off his face with a glare.

I was glad someone else was interested in having fun. Taking reality too seriously always seemed dull to me. "I've had my hair cut since that picture." The poppy seed I picked at came loose, I rolled it against the roof of my mouth with my tongue.

"My partner and I are investigating the death of a young woman that matches this description," Officer Atkinson said. "A tenant of the building recognized her and described someone like you fleeing the scene of the crime."

"I wouldn't describe what I was doing as fleeing." I didn't appreciate her implication that I was a coward.

"But you were on the roof with her?" Officer Consonant asked.

"Sure. Tried to talk her down. That's not a crime." The loose poppy seed rolled around in my mouth. I was playing a dangerous game. The black seed could get stuck back in my teeth if I wasn't careful.

"How about we take this conversation outside," Officer Atkinson suggested as she collected the contents of Gretchen's purse.

I snapped the cell phone closed and put it over the journal as she reached for it. "It's a little hot out today. I'd prefer to stay in here."

"You're in possession of evidence related to the death of a young woman. We could place you under arrest," Officer Consonant said. "Would you prefer that?"

I put the poppy seed on my lips and blew it out of my mouth. It landed on the table as I said, "depends on if your cruiser has AC."

2

The cruiser, in fact, had AC.

It blew cold air through the grated wall that separated me from the police officers. The plastic bucket seats were uncomfortable, especially since I was straddling the middle of them to read over Officer Consonant's shoulder. He sat in the driver's seat flipping through Gretchen's notebook. He read it slowly, likely having as much difficulty with the handwriting as I did.

My hands were behind my back and they'd confiscated my trench coat. I was glad to see it gone, even though I knew it'd be back soon enough. I now wore only my black T-shirt and jeans, and my skin stuck to the plastic of the seat.

They'd recited my rights to me inside the coffee shop. It took longer than I expected. We went out to their car and they stuffed me in the back. Despite that, we were still parked in front of the bakery. The flashing lights weren't helping foot traffic find its way to the bakery.

Officer Atkinson had taken my name, date of birth, and address. She radioed the information into the station from the passenger seat her door hung open into the sidewalk as if being confined in the same car as me was unacceptable.

Without an ID they had to take me at my word. But I had no reason to lie to them. I was headed out of here, likely leaving the default Todd who lived in this universe with a mess of legal problems. But he was young, college-age, and hopefully looked nothing like me. He'd get out of it easy enough.

"Why is there a description of you killing Ms. Smith in this journal?" Officer Consonant asked. His finger rested on a dog-eared page. I spotted my name at the top, the two lines of the T barely touched and the D's were bent to the left like they were playing limbo.

"You had more patience than me reading that thing. They're just dreams." I shrugged ineffectively with my hands cuffed behind my back. "Does it say I pushed her off a building?"

"Says you ran her over," he replied.

"Unit 598 we have a match on your suspect," the radio crackled out from where it was mounted on the center of the dash. "But I'm not sure you'll like it."

I grinned and licked my teeth out of habit.

"What is it?" Officer Atkinson said. When I told her my date of birth was only 20 years ago she didn't buy it but I refused to budge. I'm honest to a fault.

"Your suspect died twelve years ago," the radio replied. "At the age of eight."

I didn't meet Gretchen until high school, at least that's how it worked in all the universes I'd ever visited. If the default Todd here had died at eight then there was no way Gretchen could have known me in this universe.

"But the name and address match the death certificate," the radio continued.

"Why would you give us a dead kid's information?" Officer Atkinson asked me through the grate.

"I wanted to know what I was up to around here."

"What's that supposed to mean?" Atkinson asked.

"I think he's a stalker," Officer Consonant said. "Ms. Smith probably saw him following her and it gave her these nightmares. What's written in here is dark."

I started my focused breath. It was time to go home. Not the suburban home of my teenage self but my real home in the stars.

I slipped into the plastic valley on the passenger side of the bucket seats. I shimmied my shoulders to get comfortable and reached out for the place I wanted to go.

"Getting nervous that we're on to you?" Officer Consonant bragged. "We're going to figure out why you killed that girl."

He was more interested in answering that question than I was. I used to do it because it was predetermined by my own history. But I didn't kill her this time.

"Drop it." The slam of her car door punctuated Officer Atkinson's statement. She settled into the passenger seat "Let's run his prints at the station."

I latched onto the universe I wanted to go to, found the right time to arrive, and exhaled gently. The universe fell away once my lungs were empty.

I hope that Officer Consonant spent the rest of his life mystified by the vacant handcuffs left in his back seat.

***

Tall monitors loomed over me as I sat at the desk in my high-backed leather chair. My arms were still behind my back and I brought them forward, now free from the handcuffs. The trench coat once again hung heavy on my shoulders. My thick-soled brown leather boots did not fit the fine metal floors of the room. Especially since most humans that lived on spacecraft just wore thin-soled shoes.

If I ever meet the person in charge of picking out the outfit I wore while traveling the multiverse I'd spend some time making their life hell. It was never the right outfit for the occasion. Too hot in the summer but never quite warm enough for whatever winter I appeared in. Sure I could steal a change of clothes but that took time. Not that I had a shortage of the stuff. I just resented the unnecessary chore.

I was glad to be home. I lived at the edge of time. Long after this universe's humans went extinct. I considered the place my Fortress of Solitude, a silly reference to a childish show I liked ages ago. A younger version of me obsessed with an all-powerful hero. By now I'd put away childish obsessions.

Every timeline I visited had some version of an all-powerful hero. It rarely made great entertainment. Stories were contrived or solved in unnecessarily complicated ways. This character's name eluded me, but the name of his hideout stuck around. If only because I'd programmed it into the computer, and printed it on the side when manufacturing the satellite.

But solitude was an apt label for this location. Nothing could bother me here. So I could focus on Gretchen's recent suicide.

The tall monitor in front of me held a notification that a delivery was incoming. I ignored it and turned away from the desk, my heavy boots clomped on the shiny metal floor.

The circular room had glass windows in two opposing quadrants. One window opened out into starry space. In the opposite window a red giant star, smaller than my thumb, hung in the center.

It was Earth's sun once. But the star had betrayed its nearby satellites long ago when it expanded into its current form.

Jupiter, the planet my home orbited, would come into view in a few hours, reminding me how small I was compared to the universe around me. But even Jupiter is a spec on a telescope at a far enough distance.

The room had a recessed floor in the center with some comfortable couches. It would be a place to sit and talk with others if I ever shared this place with anyone. Instead, I used the area to lay back and think.

Counters at bar height surrounded the floor's indentation with three entryways between them and stairs that led down to the couches. Low-backed stools were pushed under the bar. The surface was intended to be used as dinner seating. But most counter space was just littered with empty glasses since I used that area to think as well. The food on this small space station wasn't worth eating, which was why I was glad to have finished the freshly baked muffin.

Six tunnels led out from the central room like a hubcap. Rooms were attached to these hallways like barnacles on an ocean ship. There were more rooms than I'd ever fill. With countless luxuries I'd never use. I had a kitchen, a spa, docks full of manufacturing equipment and tools, a gym with half a dozen workout machines I didn't know how to use, and a full-sized basketball court. The court was the most ridiculous addition because I was the only one ever on this satellite and I didn't see the fun of playing basketball by myself.

Furthest away from the center was a ring of airlocks where spaceships could dock to deliver supplies. A few ships were currently attached. Empty of deliveries and waiting to be ejected into the red giant. Based on the computer's previous notification another ship would be docked there soon.

If I ever needed supplies I went back in time and sent a ship with the necessary goods to these coordinates, and it would arrive after a few hundred years of travel. I hadn't shipped anything to myself in eons.

So whatever was on this ship would be an interesting gift from my past self.

This process never delivered anything instantly, but I didn't need speed. Occasionally, supplies were lost but in those cases, I just sent a second one. It's amazing what you can afford to do with well-placed investments and a long enough time horizon.

But there hadn't been enough time to save the Gretchen I just left. I felt bad about that, about my hand not moving fast enough. Sure, I'd killed countless Gretchens but that time was over. I'd hoped that she would live a peaceful life throughout the multiverse.

As I walked towards the center of the room I wondered how I'd heard her scream of terror through the multiverse. And why she was screaming on the ledge of a building. My multiverse traveling powers were immense but the multiverse was far larger and stranger.

Suddenly, the entire satellite began to shake. Objects floating in space shouldn't shake. Even the ship currently locked into one of the outer airlocks wouldn't move the proportionally large space station. I normally wouldn't notice it until the central computer notified me the process was complete.

I considered darting for cover and treating this like an earthquake. But I wasn't worried about something landing on my head. I rarely worried about anything; death held no consequences for me since I could fold time with my breath.

My vision began to go fuzzy from the edges. Streaks of gray and white came in from the side. It was like an old TV was unable to find a channel. Except I wasn't viewing anything through a monitor. The glasses on the table weren't clinking into each other or falling off the bar like I expected. I wondered if I was the one shaking not the room.

A long-armed humanoid figure sat at the bar across the room from me. They had no facial features or clothes. Their elbows were rested on the table holding their chin up. It was as if the shape of a person was stamped out of existence and I was looking into a starless void.

This seemed like a good time to go. I didn't know who this humanoid was or how it'd got on my space station. But there were other places in the multiverse I could be that didn't have strange void figures populating them.

I focused on my breath and reached out for another universe.

My lungs refused to inflate.

My entire chest was being compressed like I was seated in a rocket that was taking off. Or worse, as if an incessant cat sat on my chest.

The figure now had friends standing behind it. I was certain they weren't there before. It was an army of void figures. Surely I would've noticed them. Every metallic surface in the room reflected their presence. I had felt more comfortable floating through space with nothing but a tether cable connecting me to a ship than I did in front of this crowd of figures.

My heart raced but my breath didn't come. The TV static at the edges of my vision now connected across my vision like lighting connected the clouds to the Earth.

"Shouldn't be hard. Just don't go around killing innocent girls." A gentle and melodic voice said. I recognized it as Gretchen's at once.

The void figures seemed to condense into a single humanoid, like rays of light condensing through a magnifying lens. The remaining humanoid stood in front of me. Its arms were disproportionately long and came to a single point instead of a hand. Its long legs made up more than half its body. Its faceless head looked down at me. I expected the void figure to swallow me whole.

The computer sang a charming jingle, a familiar ringtone from the early years of touchscreen phones, to notify me the ship docked.

The void figure disappeared with the sound. My breath came back. I could feel a place to go but I didn't want to leave anymore, and I certainly didn't want to go there. Relieved that the figure disappeared I exhaled.

My home disappeared as I traveled through the multiverse.

3

I sat on the uncomfortably flat lid of a porcelain toilet. Humid air surrounded me and clung to my exposed neck and hands. It'd already fogged up the room's mirror. The bathroom door had a small gap in it, but it wasn't enough to relieve the room of its humidity.

Across from me, a large oval bathtub was inset into the wall. Mountains of white bubbles sat inside it.

Gretchen lay underneath the bubbles. Her blonde hair was tied in a bun and her eyes were closed. She seemed genuinely relaxed, an improvement over the last time I saw her.

However, she certainly wasn't asleep since a phone rang on the messy counter next to me. It was the same familiar ringtone I'd used on my satellite.

"Hello again." Gretchen didn't open her eyes when she spoke. "Could you shut that off?" Her speech was slow but not sloppy. She seemed to speak across a long distance and wanted to make sure the words came through clearly.

I looked at the screen, a friend, Jenna, was calling. I pressed the red decline button. Wondering if I had ever met this person.

"I didn't mean to barge in on you like this," I apologized.

Gretchen let out a small laugh through smiling lips. "I've heard that before. I'm glad I put all the bubbles I owned into the bath. Figured it'd be a nice last hurrah. But now I'm glad to have the privacy."

With a squeak, the gap in the door widened and an orange tabby cat with a fuzzy mane wandered in. It seemed to glare at me. I glared back. Unimpressed, it hopped onto the counter pushing makeup supplies out of its way as it found a seat.

"Mr. Porkchops gets angry if I take a bath with the door fully shut," Gretchen said.

"That always bothered me about cats. They're somehow independent and codependent at the same time."

Eyes still closed Gretchen let out a hum as if she was judging my words.

"You seem to be sleeping better," I said. "Do you want me to go?"

"No, not particularly. It'd be nice to have someone familiar around for my last moments."

"You're—"

The phone rang and cut me off. Gretchen lifted her hand from the water and flicked her fingertips as if to shoo the call away. She sprinkled bubbles and water onto the rug and tile floor in the process.

"I should have just left a note saying I wanted her to take care of Porkchops. Instead of a text." Gretchen shrugged. "Something to remember for next time."

"Why kill yourself? You're still so young."

Gretchen let out a throaty laugh. She turned her head and looked. She revealed bloodshot eyes and stared me down. "We both know how pointless you think life is. My nightmares make that clear."

"You're having nightmares?"

"It's how I got the sleeping pills. The doctor was worried about prescribing them to me." Gretchen grinned but the expression didn't reach her eyes. "I told him if I was going to swallow a handful of something to kill myself I'd buy a jar of peanuts.

"When it came down to it. That death felt too familiar." She rested her head back on the edge of the tub but didn't shut her eyes. She stared at the shower head mounted high on the wall.

"I'm sorry. Is there anything I can do to help?"

"You've... done enough." Her eyes slowly closed.

Plastic makeup cartridges clattered off the counter. It startled me but Gretchen was unfazed. The cat had knocked them over as he jumped down to the bathroom floor. He weaved his way out of the room.

"Was it worth it?" Gretchen asked slowly. "Was killing me so many times worth this misery that haunts me?" Her breath was deep, slow, focused, and familiar.

"It helped me learn an important lesson," I responded.

There was no hum to judge my answer.

After a moment of silence, her phone rang once again. I reached to ignore it. Rapid knocking at a door outside the room interrupted me.

I walked out of the bathroom and into the fresh air of the small apartment. I wandered through a neat bedroom and living room, filled with cheap couches and a low glass coffee table. I stood arms reach from the front door.

"Gretchen open up," Jenna said from the other side of the door. The knob rattled but the deadbolt held it shut.

I took a deep breath, focusing on my exit. I wanted to find a specific universe. One of my choosing, instead of one that called to me. I wanted a world where a default Todd knew Gretchen and she wasn't minutes away from taking her own life.

It was a tall order. But anything can be found in infinity if you look hard enough. The banging continued as I searched.

Soon I found a place that fit my parameters. I took a deep breath to leave.

"I know it's hard right now, but you don't want to do this." It sounded like Jenna was crying. "An ambulance is on the way. Come to the door."

I reached out for the deadbolt's knob. It was difficult to twist because of the pressure of Jenna trying to push it open. As soon as the bolt cleared the frame's socket the door swung open.

Jenna nearly fell into the apartment. She looked up at me through a well of tears. Her gaze lacked any recognition. Then she barreled past me.

I exhaled so she could be alone with the body of her friend.

***

I appeared in the new universe walking down a wide sidewalk next to Gretchen. The sun was bright and low in the sky and the day was still cool. It was early fall, just after midterms since Gretchen was talking about the grade she'd received on the English paper she got back in class. There seemed to be some anxiety about it, and from what I heard it was unjustified.

The architecture of the campus was a mix between newer box-shaped buildings with glass window walls and old structures with domes and slanted roofs.

The incoherent architecture was likely a consequence of the school continuing to grow for nearly a century. Someone had tried to keep the buildings matching in color so they were all uninspiring shades of desert brown. A few garden beds near the sidewalk were filled with blooming purple and yellow flowers buried in fresh dark black mulch.

Their brightness contrasted with the warm-colored leaves on the bed's trees.

We were headed towards an older-style building, with over-elaborate stone columns and a covered walkway in front of the main entrance. And I hoped we were getting some food.

I was in the body of a default Todd, the Todd that belonged to this universe, and it was hungry. I didn't have to occupy default bodies anymore, but for my current purposes, it suited me best. Two Todds in one universe would make it difficult for me to get close to Gretchen.

There was also the added benefit of not having to wear my trench coat and jeans. Today I was in a bright blue T-shirt and khaki shorts. I wore sloppy flip-flops on my feet and I thought the weather was far too cold for this. Gretchen seemed to agree in her fuzzy sage-green sweater, jeans, and black sneakers with a plastic white toe.

The whole outfit went beautifully with Gretchen's trapezoid-shaped light brown leather bag. It appeared she was smart enough to not overload it unlike me. My bag hung heavy on both my shoulders. From the straps alone I could tell it was an unfashionable and cheap multi-pocket bag. I could only assume the default Todd had filled each pocket with a library worth of textbooks.

A few other people walked past us. We weren't in the midday rush of people moving to and from classes. We may have just gotten out of a Godforsaken 8 a.m. class, and I was glad I didn't have to sit through that lecture.

This was not a college I was familiar with. When traveling through the multiverse the smallest and most inconsequential things can split a timeline in two. A person on the other side of the world could have a mole three millimeters to the left and that change would justify a split in the timeline. It'd be inconsequential to the history of the world, less important than the flap of a butterfly's wings. But it contributed to the infinite multiverse.

Small changes like that enabled me to go to the same high school every time I changed universes ages ago when I was initially investigating Gretchen's death. The layout didn't change, the teachers didn't change, and the distance from the cafeteria to the nurse's office didn't change.

But in my current effort to find a multiverse that suited my needs I had to drift from that localized cluster of similar events and find something new. Not so new that everyone spoke a different language, or had a third arm. Just new enough that the memories of the life I'd led with Gretchen fairly recently couldn't be trusted.

Details never suited me anyway. I didn't have a mind for trying to remember every little thing. The multiverse is large, and I'm lucky if I remember broad strokes. It's a necessary filtration device to keep my sanity.

But it left me flat-footed when traveling to new and strange places. Because I didn't know basic things that the default Todd would clearly know.

"How did you do on the paper?" Gretchen asked.

"Fine," I replied. For all I knew I failed it. I'd have to dig the paper out of my burdensome backpack to find out. Hell, I didn't know what my class schedule was. Was I even old enough to buy alcohol?

I recognized that I'd inherited the young adult anxieties of the default Todd but that did little to inhibit them. My powers refused to give me this Todd's memories. But it happily gave me his hormones, causing me to think like an existential college student. At least that was an improvement over acting like an immature high schooler.

"The face you made in class seemed to say differently," Gretchen said.

"Oh, well I could've done better."

"You seemed excited." She sounded like a detective trying to trap me in a corner.

"You know how I am," I replied with a shrug. Hell, she probably knew me better than I currently did.

We arrived at the entrance of the old-style columned building and I pulled open the metal door. The door seemed out of place with its small glass window, compared to the rough brick wall it was set in. Gretchen walked through and I followed as the interior opened up into a shockingly modern room.

There were a variety of tables, some big enough for eight people others for only two, on a laminate tile floor. My nose directed me towards a second room where the entrance was a metal turnstile and multiple exits were guarded by cash registers and a few cashiers. The smell of breakfast food ranging from fried meats to buttery pancakes encouraged me to believe that at least one of my problems would be solved soon.

I knew what I wanted: scrambled eggs and bacon on top of a thick waffle covered in syrup. I didn't care if it was what the default Todd normally got, I'd traveled across the multiverse, I might as well eat what I like.

The food was a step above the quality I expected from a college cafeteria, the eggs might have actually come out of a shell that morning. It was certainly better than what could be made on my space station.

Getting food went smoothly. And I devoured the pile of breakfast food with systematic efficiency. I wanted a bit of everything in each bite but my stomach didn't want to take the time to wait between bites.

Picking at her plastic clamshell bowl of yogurt with red and blue berries, Gretchen sat across from me at the four-person table, our bags took up the extra seats. The place was nearly empty this early in the morning. A few loud guys sat across the room and others filtered in from class, or more likely bed, while we ate.

"How have you been sleeping lately?" I asked as I finished off the last of my waffle. We'd been discussing something that happened last weekend or was about to happen this weekend. It wasn't particularly clear to me. The discussion was honestly one-sided since my mouth was busy with breakfast.

"Excuse me?"

"Any nightmares? Depression? Suicidal thoughts?" I felt a piece of bacon in my teeth and picked at it to get it out.

"What are you a psych major now? You hate hearing about dreams. Was discussing our plans for this weekend that unbearable for you?!"

"I'm up to go do whatever you want this weekend," I agreed hoping the default Todd was the one who would have to deliver on that promise. "I just want to make sure you're sleeping well. You know how stress from midterms and graduating and having to find a job can keep people from getting a good night's rest."

Gretchen looked at me baffled. I'd said something wrong. "It was your idea to go to the tournament this weekend. You know I don't enjoy it half as much as you. What's gotten into you lately?"

"Irritability is also a sign of poor sleep," I said.

Gretchen threw her plastic spoon into the bowl and snapped the clamshell lid closed. In a squeaky mocking tone, she said, "Irritability's a sign of bad sleep."

Pulling up the sleeve of her sweater she looked at the dainty analog gold watch on her wrist, its band was braided like hair and it hung loose only caught by the edge of her palm. "Look, I've got volleyball practice across campus and—"

"That's fine, go." I wasn't interested in waiting around in this unfamiliar life until she started having nightmares. I'd let the default Todd take over for a while and let time slip like a rope being pulled through my hands. I started breathing.

Gretchen picked up her trapezoid bag out of its chair and made room for her remaining breakfast on top of her few books and paper. "I was going to ask if you wanted to... are you okay?"

"Yeah, just medi—" Gray fuzz appeared at the edge of my vision. I looked around trying not to lose the focus of my breath. For better or worse I couldn't lose focus, because my lungs were caught in place.

A black void figure sat in the chair that recently held Gretchen's bag. I looked to Gretchen. Her eyes were wide in shock, but the rest of her face hadn't seemed to update and share the expression.

Then every chair in the food court that wasn't occupied by a person was filled by a void figure. Void figures stood behind the few unattended cash registers. The counters where food was served had a long caterpillar line of void figures packed together as close as possible.

They had no faces but it felt like every single one was staring directly at me. Regardless of whether their chair faced me or not. It was like staring down a wild animal as it decided to lunge or flee.

The gray static at the edge of my vision connected in the center.

Every void figure fell out of its chair and collapsed into a single figure that loomed behind Gretchen. She still held her bag frozen in time while placing yogurt inside. The lean figure dwarfed her by at least two head lengths.

Gretchen's pupils seemed to be pressed against the corner of her eye as if she were trying to look over her shoulder.

The void figure disappeared. Gretchen shrieked. She dropped her bag and bowl on the ground, spilling fruit and white yogurt all over the leather bag.

I covered my ears and lost my focus.

A few others in the food court turned to look, startled from their peaceful breakfast. Most turned away after seeing the spilled yogurt, likely categorizing the shriek as an overreaction to the mess.

"Did you see those people?" she asked in a hushed tone.

"Yep." I wasn't sure which was more startling. Having them stare at me with their empty faces or sharing the experience with Gretchen.

"Did anyone else?"

I shrugged, got up, and walked towards the closest occupied table. Three guys with messy hair, loose-fitting shirts, and gym shorts sat around talking about something on a phone. They looked like they just got out of bed. Gretchen gave me a look like I was crazy but I didn't care what these people thought of me.

"Did you see a bunch of strange humanoid figures sit in all the seats in here a moment ago?"

"Only strange humanoid I see is you," one replied while the others laughed.

"Thanks." I grabbed a pile of brown napkins they had on their table and turned back to Gretchen. She'd need more than cheap recycled paper to get the fruit stains out but it was a start.

"Seems like just us," I told her.

"Well if I didn't have nightmares before I will now." She forced out a laugh while picking up juicy red strawberries off the light colored bag. "Since when did you get comfortable talking to random people?"

"You know me."

"I'm starting to have my doubts." She dropped the last of the dirty napkins into the plastic container. The bag was far from clean but it was the best that could be done. "Walk me to practice?" She sounded shaken by the void figure's appearance. Any fight we were about to have was forgotten.

"Sure," I agreed. But that was work default Todd could easily take care of. I slipped my backpack over my shoulder. While we walked out of the food court I began to focus my breaths to jump ahead in this timeline.

Except my mind was unable to grasp anything in the multiverse.

4

I sat on a green metal bench outside the university's gym where Gretchen and I had parted ways a few hours ago. The contents of my bulky backpack were splayed out on the bench and ground around me. Textbooks, notebooks, a computer as thick as my wrist, along with a dozen nicknacks like pens, wallet, keys, wired mouse, thumb drives, and an empty granola bar wrapper.

The gym was a boxy building with glass windows at the front. It sat at the edge of campus. Across a wide five-lane road were old blue and white houses that didn't match the school's design. Small campus streets, which hardly had more than a few busses drive down them, sat on the other side of campus.

There was a bit of a green park between the gym and the rest of the campus but it wasn't big enough to do much more than have a picnic. Campus buildings were short and squat and the long walk from our breakfast to here told me wherever we were land was not an issue. Which meant that this was not anywhere close in the multiverse to the place I got a lemon poppyseed muffin.

Aside from sizing up the campus, I'd learned a lot about myself in the past few hours. Unfortunately, the first thing I discovered was that even when I sat still and let my mind focus on my breath I still couldn't travel through time.

The next thing I learned was that I cared about what people thought of me when I couldn't just escape to somewhere new or hide alone in my satellite. And since it was now past midday the sun was out and plenty of people were headed to and from class. Most of them at least made cursory glances towards the guy in flip-flops with a mess of schoolwork claiming a bench.

I learned little about this particular default Todd. The university's name was Wigham Technical University. Names of states, countries, and cities rarely stayed consistent through the multiverse, a place's name, much like a rose's, had little to do with its properties. I suspected I was in the southern part of the United States, since despite the fall leaves on the trees I was glad to be in shorts and a T-shirt as the sun wound up high in the sky.

The wallet and keys, while valuable long term, were currently useless. There was no cash and only a few cards. The student ID could get me some food, I used to buy breakfast following Gretchen's lead. But long term I had no idea how much money this guy had. The car could be parked anywhere, and the keys were so cheap that it didn't have a fob to locate it, even if I somehow got close.

I studied, or at least was taking a class in computer graphic design and ethics. Neither of which personally interested me. Both books were dog-eared and marked up, leading me to believe that either the default Todd was interested, or had bought them used from someone who was.

The computer and phone would have actually useful information on them. Like my bank account balance, phone numbers of friends, and maybe directions on how to get to the address on my driver's license. However, those were locked. This universe hadn't advanced enough to use biometrics to log in and none of the passwords I tried worked.

To make matters worse that wasn't even the most devastating thing I learned. One of the last things I pulled out of the bag was a doll, of a superhero. It immediately got buried back into the bag.

If Gretchen had left the gym I hadn't noticed her. Without access to a phone, I had no way to call or contact her. She was the only person I knew in this universe. If this default Todd had friends I wouldn't recognize them. I was alone in a foreign universe. Not only stranded but with nothing but this backpack's contents to my name.

I closed my eyes and took a deep breath like I was going to travel. I hoped it would at least calm me down. It was ineffective at both.

I spent all morning trying to come up with a plan. Every single one of them included Gretchen. And I'd misplaced her. And it wasn't like she was going to come wandering back to me.

"Hey, Todd."

I opened my eyes. Gretchen stood in front of me looking down at me with her hazel eyes. Her hair was pulled back in a ponytail and she was wearing a purple T-shirt with 'Wigham Tech Volleyball' written on it in a blocky gold font.

"What's all this?" She asked gesturing at the bench I'd covered in backpack contents.

"My stuff," I replied.

"Yeah, that was obvious when I saw Xiomara." She let out a cute laugh under her breath. "Why's it on the bench?" She checked her wristwatch. "Don't you have class right now?"

"Yeah, I missed it. Can we talk?" I pushed the textbooks to the side so she could sit down.

"Jenna and I are going to lunch," she poked a thumb behind her at Jenna who had short brunette hair and a gym bag slung over her shoulder cutting through the purple 'Wigham Tech Volleyball' lettering on her white shirt. "You need to get to class. You've got that ethics test. Is everything okay?"

"No." I looked down at the deflated backpack between my feet. "Things are pretty far from okay."

"You'll feel better after the test." She picked the backpack up off the sidewalk. "Pack this up, go to class. You'll do fine on it even if you're a little late. You studied all night for it." Jenna readjusted her gym bag impatiently. "We can talk later. Let me know how your test went."

"How do I get to..." I opened up my wallet and recited the address on my license.

"You're going home?" she asked shocked.

"Like after the test. I'd like to go home and relax."

"Yeah. But all the way there? We've got the tournament this weekend."

"Sure, sure, we can still do that."

"Not if you're at your parent's place 3 hours away." Gretchen smiled like I'd told a joke but her tone sounded worried.

"Oh." I had less information than I thought.

"Look, you go to class, I'll get lunch with Jenna, and we'll meet at the SUB in an hour and a half."

"SUB?"

"Student union building..." Jenna injected impatiently.

"It's where we got breakfast," Gretchen added. "Do you need to go to a doctor?"

"No, I'm fine. I'll go to class. See you at the SUB in a bit." I waved them away.

Gretchen leaned down and kissed me on the forehead. "You'll do great on the test don't worry!"

"Thanks." I piled my books up sliding them into the backpack. I had no intention to take the test, even if I knew where the classroom was.

***

Finding the Student Union Building was more difficult than I expected. Retracing my steps around a brand-new college campus was not simple. Directions were never my strong suit, hence why I mostly lived in more advanced timelines with decent navigational technology.

At one point in my search for the SUB, I found myself on small sidewalks behind old buildings where putrid dumpsters were stored. I was lost, not just in the multiverse but, on a simple college campus. It was embarrassing.

When Gretchen started calling me to figure out where I was I found a busy area and asked someone for directions. Asking wasn't as easy as normal. My hand started shaking and my chest felt like my shirt was too tight. I asked, so Gretchen wouldn't have to wait too long for me. Despite looking at me as if I was asking what color the sky was they pointed me in the right direction and I eventually saw the old columned building.

I walked into the familiar food court area, but Gretchen wasn't there. I couldn't call her without access to my phone so I stood near the door taking my heavy backpack off to let my shoulders rest. It didn't take long. I picked up the call immediately. She asked where I was and I told her.

"Why are you down there?" She asked. "I told you to meet me in the study lounge upstairs."

She had said that while I was still lost on campus. It didn't mean anything at the time and still didn't. "Can you come get me?" I could explore the place but based on my navigation around the campus I doubted that'd be successful.

"Sure." She agreed without any annoyance. "Are you still not doing well? We can go somewhere with fewer people." Her voice was kind and gentle and felt like a buoy in a storm.

The SUB was much busier than this morning. Nearly every table had people and the rest had trash that needed to be cleared away. "This place is fine. I just... it'll be easier to explain."

"I understand." She was genuine, her voice didn't sound like a rote reply. Which was characteristic of all the Gretchens I'd ever met.

Gretchen found me easily enough. I was the only person standing still at the front door, everyone else that came through the door walked with a purpose. Holding my hand, more like a parent than a partner, she led me through the busy building. We walked down a few tiled hallways with storefronts that sold books, apparel, and school supplies. It was like a tiny mall.

An old brick stairwell sat off the main path and it smelled musty. Whoever renovated the place found it easier to leave the thing buried rather than update it with the rest of the building. We walked up and I was glad I'd asked Gretchen to get me, otherwise, I'd never find this hidden corridor.

At the top of the stairs sat some vending machines and bathrooms. This floor was not all hallways and stores. It was wide open, only broken up by thick pillars painted white, gold, and purple. Small glass half-walls let you look down at the food court. Unlike the hallways downstairs this felt like a place I could breathe.

The center of the room had a few wooden tables, along with a purple pool table and two folded ping pong tables made makeshift walls around it. I wouldn't be surprised if the ping pong tables were a matching royal purple once unfolded.

Countless couches and chairs were littered around the room. They were upholstered in easy-to-clean vinyl that matched the school's colors. Each cushioned seat had a small swivel desk inserted into the arm.

Study rooms surrounded the perimeter. Their glass walls made the students inside look like fish in a tank.

Gretchen's trapezoid bag still splotched with the muted red remnants of a strawberry, sat on a couch near the corner. A paperback novel sat on the swivel desk next to a clear plastic cup of light brown iced coffee. She led me there still holding my hand as we sat down.

"How are you doing?" She asked gently.

"I've been better." I stated it flatly; disappointed in myself for my inabilities. Normally, even if I couldn't find my way out of a paper bag, I was at least a guy who could navigate the multiverse. Now I couldn't even do that.

Gretchen squeezed my hand. "Did the test not go well? Are you nervous about the tournament?"

"The things we saw this morning." I took a deep breath to gather my courage. It reminded me I couldn't travel and my exhalation deflated me.

"Yeah, that was strange." Gretchen sounded as if she had to heave the memory from the back of her mind.

"I can travel the multiverse with my breath." I jumped in with two feet, without holding my breath. "I've lived countless lifetimes as every kind of person there is. I know it sounds wild but I've been to the future and past and a bunch of parallel universes where we've dated and gone to different colleges. But now I can't do it anymore."

Gretchen laughed, not to mock me but like she was in on a joke with me. "Like Prisoner 174?"

I looked at her confused.

"Maybe it was a different number after his name." She continued with a smile despite my clear confusion. "You just described Prisoner 174 from the Cosmos Chronicles. You showed it to me... I don't know a year ago?"

"I'm not the Todd you've known since high school. I'm a Todd from a parallel universe."

"So you don't know the name of the captain from Sapphire?" She took a drink of her coffee.

"No, I don't."

"What would you say if I said: I've always thought that it would've made more sense for the eagles to fly the ring to Mordor." She looked at me with a playful smile.

"Whatever you're going on about I don't understand." Gretchen usually was more receptive to these conversations. I'd had a couple of them with her over my lifetimes.

"You're serious." Gretchen's face turned to apprehension. "There's no urge in you to tell me that it was about the journey and how the eagles are apathetic to the wars of men and a dozen other excuses?"

"I have the urge to travel forward in time to skip this part of the conversation."

"You can do that?"

"Not anymore." I rubbed my head in frustration.

"Because of the things we saw this morning?"

"Currently they're my main suspect. Although these powers didn't come with an instruction book."

"Todd would love this, it's classic Cosmos Chronicles. I just hope you're not an asshole like Prisoner 174."

"In what ways was he an asshole?" I asked hesitantly.

"Just pessimistic and nihilistic and in general didn't care about anyone but himself because," she waved her hands in the air and in a mockingly deep voice she said, "in the grand scheme of things it didn't matter."

"Being immortal and jumping through time will give you that sense of perspective."

Gretchen laughed genuinely. "You're not messing with me? This isn't a bit?" As she sucked the last of her coffee her straw made a loud slurping sound. "Because you know you should have fairy cake and not a sense of perspective."

"What do cupcakes have to do with anything? I genuinely don't understand half the stuff you're saying."

"Is this how Todd feels trying to keep me up to speed?" She groaned to herself. "Cosmos Chronicles is this old British sci-fi show where the main character has a motorbike that can travel through time and space. He always has a companion that rides on the back of the bike with him and they investigate crimes through the galaxy.

"His catchphrase, or whatever, was basically when traveling through the expansiveness of time and space the last thing you should hold onto is your perspective. Because of how small you clearly are in it. He always said you should hold onto fairy cakes though because they're delicious."

"I'm more partial to muffins," I said with a grin.

"So was Prisoner 174," Gretchen replied with a slight scowl. "But now you've taken over my boyfriend's body. I can't just exorcise you to get him back?"

"I spent most of the morning trying my normal method of traveling without any luck."

"Which is why you were on the bench and late to class. Wait, how did you do on the ethics test if you don't have his memories?" She looked at her drink, saw it was empty, then tilted it to slurp the last watery drops of coffee out. "Did you even go?!"

"I didn't."

"Oh come on!" She slammed her drink down in frustration, the ice rattled against the plastic. "That test was important to you... him... whatever. Todd spent all last night studying."

"What's one night in the grand scheme of eternity?"

"No! You don't get to just belittle our short mortal lives because you're... are you immortal or just long-lived?"

"If I die I usually reincarnate in a universe similar to one I died in."

"What happens to the home Todd in that situation? The Todd whose body you died in... or the one you're reincarnated in for that matter."

"I call them default Todds. And I usually don't go back to to find out."

"Okay, so. Ground rules for this universe: don't get my Todd killed, injured, maimed, addicted to anything, or involved with shady individuals. Second, don't keep screwing him over. I can take you to his apartment and help you study, but he better have as good, if not better, grades than when you showed up.

"That shouldn't be hard for a wise immortal like yourself. If you mess up his GPA he'll be an anxious mess. And while I will help him through it, I'll be plotting ways to hunt you down, multiverse traveler or not."

For a moment, with the look in her eyes, I believed she could do it.

"Can you do that?" She asked.

"I'll do my best, but I do have other reasons for being here." I wasn't expecting to have to reveal myself to Gretchen this soon, or at all. "And this is my body, not yours, so I don't see why you get to make the rules."

"Unlike you, I actually care about what happens to this body. And whatever else you have going on, you can do it between studying. After all," Gretchen grinned and with a mocking tone said, "What's one night of studying in the grand scheme of eternity."

I didn't appreciate the perspective.

"Come on," she patted my knee and stood up gathering her things to go. "I'll take you home and get you set up with his class schedule. You can call me if you have any problems."

"Not unless you know the code to Todd's phone," I said as I lifted the heavy backpack over my shoulder. Most of the weight was the computer, and it was practically useless to me.

"No I don't, and if I did he wouldn't appreciate me giving it out to a stranger."

"I'm not a stranger! I'm him." I'd lived countless lifetimes with Gretchen. She'd always been accepting of me. Replacing the default Todd had always been simple, but this universe was unsettlingly different.

Gretchen tossed her empty cup into a trashcan. "You are far stranger than you realize." She smiled and then frowned. "Damn, Todd would've loved that reference."

5

The walk to the apartment was long and balmy in the afternoon sun. The morning's chill was long gone. Despite the warmth, I still regretted the flip-flops I wore since they did little to protect my feet from bumps and cracks in the ground. Plus they kept slipping off my toes every hundred yards or so. I planned to find a good pair of socks and shoes first thing in the apartment, instead of these hazards.

To enter the apartment we passed through the iron gate after Gretchen pinned in a code on a keypad. The apartment was comprised of multiple buildings all designed to look like homes with their angled roofs and wooden slat siding. But the height of the three-story buildings and concrete stairs cutting through the middle ruined the illusion. Flags of all different colors hung in various windows, some purple and gold, others bright yellow or rainbow.

Covered parking spots, made with corrugated roofing on thick beams, sat in front of the building that Gretchen led me towards. There were a few motorcycles and scooters parked under the shelter, chained to the thick beam.

After climbing a few flights of stairs Gretchen showed me which key belonged to the door. I could have figured it out through trial and error. I didn't appreciate being so dependent on her.

I opened the door and I was immediately greeted by the scent of a cedar forest. A few candles were lit around the kitchen and living room. Dangerous to keep them unattended but it was likely better than the default smell of a college apartment.

To my immediate left was a galley kitchen. Surprisingly neat considering there were no robots to automatically clean things. A few bags of chips, bread, and fruit lay out on the counter next to a tabletop microwave. An old coil-style stove oven combo was inset into the counter. It seemed to be giving off heat and the smell of pizza did its best to fight through the candle's aroma. A black fridge hummed in the corner and liquor bottles rattled on top of it.

Directly in front of me behind a bar-height counter barely big enough for two people was the living room. Past the living room was a floor-to-ceiling window that ran the majority of the wall. The window was blocked by a brown futon with a thick pad.

I wouldn't want to sleep on the thing, it seemed lumpy in the worst ways, but would suit an intoxicated guest ready to pass out. Across from it, nearly blocking the entrance to the living room was a short entertainment center. A blank flat-screen television, game console and controllers sat on the stand next to a few action figures and model spaceships, which I didn't think would hold up in space if ever built at full size.

I never expected a college apartment to be so well taken care of. Posters were tacked up on the wall. Some were maps of places I'd never heard of. Others were movie posters with square-jawed heroes shooting lasers with one hand and clutching a damsel in another.

I turned to Gretchen, who'd followed me in, to comment on my surprise, when I saw where the mess was hiding. Behind her, opposite the kitchen, a long six-person table, that would be incapable of seating anyone in its current state, was covered in clothes, cloth and an open toolbox. A sewing machine sat at the far end of the table in a dark corner that had no window. A cheap floor lamp with a post no bigger than my finger sat next to it turned off, its cylindrical white lampshade was stained with pale blue splotches.

At the edge of the table next to the door was a turquoise and neon green bug-eyed alien with lumpy folds around its cheeks, forehead, and chin. It looked at me with glossy black eyes and white pupils, unblinking. Its mouth was open, hanging off the edge of the table, looking like it'd been decapitated in shock.

I pointed over Gretchen's shoulder. "What the hell is that?"

"Oh, that's Lieutenant Traktar. It should be dry by now." She lifted the head off the table gently and placed it over her own. It took up most of the width of her shoulders and her blonde hair poked out the bottom around her neck. The flabby face looked out of place on Gretchen's athletic frame.

She pulled at some clear wires and the mask's mouth moved up and down. With her other hand, she pulled on a wire that made the eyes glance back and forth.

My look of shock must have been entertaining because Gretchen's laugh came through a bit muted by the mask. She let go of the puppet wire and the eyes rolled in opposite directions.

"It's a little loose on me." She wiggled the head back and forth, it jostled on her shoulders adding to the unsettling image. "But it should fit your head just fine."

"No thanks," I said as she took it off and set it back on the table.

"You're going to have to finish this costume for the tournament this weekend. You were going to come here and work on it right after the test. Or at least Todd was."

"I can't finish all that." Walking to the table and leafing through the piles of cloth I found printouts of the alien lieutenant and paper sewing patterns. "Let alone wear it."

"You said you lived a bunch of different lives. I assumed at least one of them was as a master tailor. At the very least I'm sure you were an actor who could don a costume."

"That was ages ago," I ruffled through the cloth and paper. The images were from all different angles of the character. Some he was standing next to the square-jawed hero from the living room's posters.

"That's fine this was a seventies sci-fi TV show. The acting standards aren't that high. But this weekend is the biggest Galaxy Gang convention in the world. Todd's been working on this for months. I'm not letting you flub it three days away."

"Galaxy Gang?"

"Like I said the standards weren't that high. But it's pretty popular and there's a reboot movie coming out next year—"

"Shouldn't've brought up the movie," I heard someone say from behind me.

I turned around to see a tall man set a beeping phone down on the bar. He wore a durag over his hair and a white tank top. Turning off the beeping phone he walked into the kitchen. "We're going to have to listen to why the new guy isn't going to be able to replace John Atkinson because what is it again?" He looked at me while he pulled the pizza out of the oven.

I looked back with a blank stare.

"He doesn't have the same bravado of character," Gretchen replied.

"You feeling okay Todd?" He cut the pizza with a large knife not waiting for it to cool.

"He's just stressed, Murphy." Gretchen looked at me. "There's lots of work to do on the outfit."

"Well don't have too much fun." Murphy sounded like he doubted the possibility and loaded up his plate with half the pizza. "I'm going out later tonight so don't worry about keeping me up," he said before disappearing back to his room.

"I have a roommate?" I asked in a hushed tone to Gretchen.

She shrugged and opened a door that was next to the table, it led to a bedroom with walls covered in nerdy posters. "You thought you lived alone? You're in college."

"I kinda thought we'd live together."

Gretchen laughed like a bell. "My father would never pay for that. I live on the other side of the complex though. Let me show you where Todd keeps his school notes and stuff."

"I thought there was lots to do on the outfit?" I said with a mocking smile.

"There is," she looked serious. "But Murphy'd be suspicious if I was showing you how to put it together."

I followed her into the bedroom and she showed me around Todd's room. It was the most thorough, and only tour, I'd ever gotten of my own stuff. And while I would've preferred to rummage around the default Todd's things unsupervised, it was helpful to understand what half the junk was since Gretchen seemed intent on me not screwing up his life.

She showed this intention by not leaving my side until the wee hours of the night. We made little progress on the outfit. My sewing skills were centuries old at this point and memories still faded with time for me. Her understanding of the project was the broad strokes Todd had given her when they were hanging out in the evenings.

She left late at night yawning and, after having me repeat the time and location of Todd's morning class, she went home. I went to lay on Todd's bed immediately expecting a dreamless slumber I'd been so used to.

Instead, I had a dream.

***

I woke up startled by the phone on the bedside table that rang incessantly. Ignoring the call, it was unsurprisingly Gretchen, I tried to hold the dream in my memory. Most of the details had already become fuzzy, but a sentence remained in my mind. I repeated it to myself while I found something to capture it with.

The ethics notebook Gretchen was reviewing with me last night was no longer on the desk. It'd been replaced by a large drawing tablet. I checked Todd's backpack and found the notebook. I flipped to a page towards the back and grabbed the pen that sat next to the tablet.

It wrote nothing since it was a stylus. These valleys of time where people hadn't fully moved away from the old tech and converted to the new could be frustrating. If biometrics had been introduced, I could scan my finger or face on the tablet and write on that. But I was locked out of anything useful.

A 32 oz souvenir cup with scenes of medieval adventures and two knights staring at each other sat on the desk filled with pens. I pulled one out and checked the tip to verify it wasn't a stylus. The tip looked like a fine paintbrush, but I didn't care at this point. I jotted down the words that the dream left me with. It was all I had of this rare experience.

Hold Gretchen. Don't let go. Especially when she overshadows you.

The letters were swished back and forth because of the bristles of the pen's tip. The words seemed so important one minute ago. The sentence made no sense to me. Through my chaotic dream, they were the idea I kept learning, kept repeating, and kept urging myself to remember.

The dream experience was familiar, I was pushed from world to world. Like flipping through cable channels, except each one was a different universe.

Default Todd's phone rang again. I looked at the clock. 6:30 am. Five hours of sleep seemed to feel like ten. Todd didn't have class until 11 today, I had time. Muting the phone's ringing I tried to breathe and travel again.

My breath latched on to nothing.

The phone rang a third time. I picked up the call noticing a small pebble-like flip phone next to it. That wasn't in Gretchen's very thorough tour of the room last night.

"I'm outside I don't want to knock and wake Murphy up. You ready Lieutenant?"

"It's not even light outside, we just went to bed. What's going on?"

Gretchen groaned in frustration. "Is this other Todd? Let me in. I thought we got rid of you."

"Got rid of me?!" I didn't appreciate being the other, if anything I was the main Todd since I was able to travel the multiverse. Or at least could at some point in time.

Trudging to the front door I opened it to reveal Gretchen wearing an outfit that did not fit in this time and place.

Her face was painted green except the area around her eyes which was her natural skin tone. Her lips appeared bright red, not from lipstick, just from the contrast against the green paint. The paint went all the way down her neck and around her ears, all exposed since her hair was tied up in tight braids with dozens of bobby pins.

She wore an old leather jacket with bright military-style patches and dark brown splotches that looked like scorch marks. Under the jacket, she wore a white crop top, a little stained by green at the bottom since her midriff was painted to match her face.

A belt hung loose around her waist with leather pouches tacked on it and a holster with a sci-fi gun handle sticking out. Her pants looked like armor, but upon further inspection, they were painted foam tacked to tight jeans. The black leather boots and gloves didn't quite match the outfit, but they didn't detract either.

Gretchen didn't look like any alien I'd ever seen outside of television. But her outfit would fit in well on the set of any network TV show.

She shooed me into the bedroom, and I felt underdressed in the gym shorts and t-shirt I'd apparently worn as pajamas.

"I need you to leave." Gretchen's voice was firm and she loomed over me as I sat at the edge of the bed.

"Go? But you just got here." I cracked a grin.

Gretchen glared at me. "You weren't here yesterday or the day before and we've been having a nice time without you. Despite Todd having to convince his professor to let him retake the test you skipped."

"The university doesn't consider a multiverse traveler possessing his body a valid excuse?"

"You left," she pressed a gloved hand to her green forehead, "leave again. Why'd you have to come back today? If you're a time traveler then you can just pop in whenever. Maybe after finals, or better yet, never."

"I didn't go anywhere, or at least I didn't mean to."

She looked at me skeptical then noticed green paint on the fingertips of her glove. She groaned. Her skin tone poked through the green paint making three little dots on her forehead. "I put all this makeup on and Todd isn't even here to appreciate it."

"Men, am I right?"

"How'd you leave?" She asked. My joke did little to soften her glare. "Why can't you leave again? Let's figure this out before it's time to go." She looked at the clock on the bedside table. "Or at least before we're too late for the tournament."

"I went to sleep then woke up here three days later. That's it. Hell, I thought it was still Thursday. We're not going to fix it in a morning."

"Great! That means sleep makes you slip through time. Go to sleep again," she gestured for me to lay down on Todd's bed.

"I can't just go to sleep. I feel like I've been asleep for ages."

"Wait, you don't feel like we stayed up until three?"

"You're here at 6:30 and you were up until 3 a.m.? What were you doing?"

"None of your business," Gretchen barked.

"Three hours of sleep, less considering all the face paint." I noticed dark purple bags under her eyes where paint hadn't been applied yet. "Are you sleeping okay?"

"We're not focusing on my problems; we're focused on yours." She walked to the closet, a small inset in the wall covered by a sliding door made of mirrors, and pulled out an outfit. "Put this on."

It was the finished Lieutenant Traktar outfit. A leather vest and blue jumpsuit hung neatly on the hanger. A construction tool belt with big pockets typically used for nails was looped around the hook of the hanger. She laid the outfit on the bed then returned to the closet and pulled out a box. She placed it on the desk chair and started unpacking it. The first thing she lifted out of it was Traktar's head. She set the mask on the desk and its glossy black eyes with white pupils stared at me.

"Come on hurry up," she said when she saw I was still sitting on the bed. "It's not like I haven't seen that body naked before." She continued to pull out pieces of foam armor from the box.

"Why do you even want to go to this tournament thing? You said you weren't going to enjoy it. The default Todd isn't here to enjoy it either. God knows I won't."

"Stop calling him that!" She placed a bit of foam armor on Traktar's blubbery head. "We aren't some stale crackers you can keep throwing away."

"What do you mean keep?"

"Look, I don't care if you think time and all these little rote things us mortals do is meaningless, but we're going to the convention. It's important to Todd. It's important to me." Her eyes began to well with tears. "Just do your best to try not to constantly remind me that you're not him."

"You just don't strike me as someone who... I don't know would be so into this stuff. It's all made up and you're trying to imitate it so thoroughly." I gestured to the posters on the wall and small figurines on Todd's desk. Then realized I could've pointed to anything in the room to make my point. "Hell you said def— Todd would enjoy this more than you."

"I said that because I was in a bad mood and he, no, you were being aloof." The well of tears flowed over and she grabbed a tissue from the bedside table. Looking in the mirror she dabbed the tears away trying to protect her face paint. "You don't get it that's fine. I didn't either."

I decided to start pulling on the jumpsuit, reluctant to upset her further. "If I'm going to have a shot at acting like your boyfriend, then maybe you can help me understand."

"We've been going to this convention since I could drive." Her voice quivered but wasn't full sobs. "These costumes are the fourth or fifth version we've made. That mask alone took most of winter break to put together. We had fun doing it and this is our reward for the effort."

"I understand investing time in things to make them precious." It was why the life I'd lived with Gretchen after saving her in high school was so meaningful. But all the following ones fell apart. Although usually not as spectacular as my relationship with this Gretchen. I'd never felt like so much of an outsider.

"It's more than that. There's an energy to these events. I played soccer and volleyball and did gymnastics because I liked the energy of the crowd and the team. But there's competition in all that crap. At a convention, everyone's on the same team. You put on a costume, walk around with other nerds, and take pictures with people who love the character you're dressed as. When it's over you practically believe you're the character you're dressed as, headed out to her spaceship in the parking lot."

I shrugged the vest on over my jumpsuit and looked at the armor on the desk, not sure what to do next. "I'll try not to ruin your day," I said. "If I could leave and give you your Todd back I would. I didn't mean to show up and ruin your life."

Gretchen chuckled at my last comment as if she was in on some joke.

It made me wonder how much she knew.

6

Gretchen explained most of the key information about my character on the drive to the convention center. I was a biology officer on the Independence, the exploration ship that the Galaxy Gang TV show was set on. I was a minor star of the show and was involved in missions to research planets that the USS Independence discovered.

She was dressed as Galdot a character the writers introduced in a later season as a love interest of Traktar. In her opinion, Galdot's sole purpose was to be killed off in the season finale to get Traktar to come up with a clever solution to defeat the alien race the Independence had fought all season. She said Todd was unwilling to admit this himself, but she seemed confident he would see her reasoning after a few more viewings.

What Gretchen hadn't explained was the trivia tournament that I was supposed to compete in that afternoon.

Which is why I was sweating under the stage lights that shone down on us, look out to a dwindling audience. I'd taken the Traktar mask off multiple rounds ago, my hair was wet with sweat from the day in general. I had no clue how Gretchen hadn't sweat through her makeup yet.

Gretchen certainly hadn't shared enough about the show for me to be competitive. That had yet to become a problem since we were on a team with Todd's high school friends. Despite sitting back in my chair rather than hunching over the buzzers like everyone else on stage, our team still advanced through the rounds.

The tournament was held in an auditorium. The audience was mostly other people competing in the trivia contest which led to the audience shrinking every time a team was knocked out. Every time the lanky announcer asked an esoteric question about the 50-year-old show in his nasally voice my envy for the losers grew.

My teammates were unfamiliar. Old friends of Todd's that met up at this convention every year and occasionally on school breaks. But I never really focused on his friends when I revisited high school. Navigating other people's relationships was difficult, Gretchen in this universe was a prime example. But we'd spent most of the morning with them, and to avoid breaking Gretchen's immersion of the convention I learned their names.

Nick sat to my right and closest to the team we were facing off against in this quarter-final round of the tournament. He was a stocky guy with light blond hair and was the only one in the group not wearing a costume.

So far I hadn't enjoyed my time with him. He seemed to stick up his nose at any uncertified merchandise we'd seen on the floor, spouting on about copyright law which I doubted was a course in the IT degree he was pursuing.

He was critical of anyone walking around with what he called Great Value cosplay. This was one of many inside jokes I hadn't looped into yet. However, his tone made it clear the comment was not a compliment. He hadn't said anything about our costumes but I had no doubt he'd easily find an issue if we weren't "friends."

Gretchen sat to my left, still painted green. The makeup now covered her eyelids and the dark sacks under her eyes. She also added a bright pink wig just before going into the convention center. The wig's hair was barely long enough to reach her shoulders.

Between my remarkable mask and Gretchen's approachable smile, it was no shock that by lunch I'd forgotten how many pictures we'd posed in.

Past Gretchen was Justin and Julia. They were also in a matching Galaxy Gang cosplay, both as humans. Their jumpsuits fit loosely and they didn't have as many badges as Lieutenant Traktar.

Gretchen used a term I'd forgotten to explain they weren't specific characters from the show but dressed to match what characters would wear in the fictional universe. Nick's opinion, openly, was that this was better than doing a crappy imitation of a well-known character and getting laughed at. I suspected if they were strangers he'd sing a different song.

We sat at a long table with a white cloth over it facing the dwindling crowd. Red buzzers sat in front of each of us. We'd done well enough to make it to the quarter-finals. The matchups consisted of nine questions, whoever answered five of them right moved on to the next round.

Our team typically won before the seventh question. I had yet to use my buzzer since none of the questions were as simple enough to be covered in Gretchen's crash course. Despite that something in the back of my mind urged me to buzz before the question was even finished. It was like my fingers had the muscle memory, I just lacked any memory of the show.

Maybe my fingers wanted to participate as part of the team, a sentiment I didn't share. Maybe they just wanted to buzz in so I'd quit having to hear Nick give me a hard time about not answering questions between rounds. Unshockingly, sitting out of trivia was not a characteristic of the default Todd.

However, Nick didn't give anyone else on the team a hard time for being quiet. Justin and Julia had buzzed twice each and I noticed Gretchen was buzzing too late, always seeming to be a second behind Nick or the other team.

I decided to give in to my finger's request. A little bored, a little interested in stirring the pot.

The announcer asked most of the sixth question, something about some fictional interspace law. I didn't know or care, I tapped a buzzer before he could finish.

The buzzer belonged to Gretchen.

The announcer cut himself off and looked at Gretchen.

"Um, that's article 19 from the revised Kremulon contract," Gretchen replied.

"Correct." The announcer confirmed.

Justin and Julia cheered from the end of the table. We'd answered our fifth question correctly and advanced to the semi-finals. I sat back and clapped. Both Gretchen and Nick glared at me.

I continued to clap but added a smile and shrug.

***

"Look we're never going to win this thing if you keep hogging the buzzer," I said to Nick.

We were huddled in the center aisle near the back of the auditorium where it sloped up to give the back seats a good view of the stage. The last two teams of the quarter-finals faced off on stage. The houselights still shone, but they were dim compared to the bright stage lights. I'd found a cool place under a vent, glad to feel its breeze on my neck.

"I wouldn't need to hog it if you'd buzz in and pull your weight," Nick retorted.

"Trust me you don't want me buzzing in," I said. "Gretchen has watched enough of the show with me to know most of the answers." I turned to Gretchen, "You just need to buzz in quicker."

Nick groaned and a few people from the team seated near us looked over, obviously interested in hearing the questions not our quibble. They should've sat closer if they cared.

"Todd's right. He's always said winning trivia is buzzer management," Justin said. "Don't wait until you know the answer to buzz in."

"You know more about this show than her," Nick said. "I don't see why you're being an asshole and putting the weight of the team on me. Is it just so your girlfriend can get some glory?"

"Yeah because winning this dumb trivia game is practically a Nobel prize."

"Who are you, man?" Nick glared at me and stomped off to sit in a row to wait for our next round.

Justin and Julia followed him and Gretchen and I sat near them. The chairs were hinged so that they folded out once you sat on them. Mine squeaked loudly under me.

I carefully balanced the Traktar helmet on the seat next to me and leaned over to Gretchen.

"I thought you said you like these things because they weren't competitive?" I whispered.

"I do." She responded in a hushed tone. "It's just that Nick's been signing us up for this the past few years. He really wants to win it."

"And your Todd?"

"Likes supporting his friends," she said. "So don't mess up his life by ruining his friendship by arguing with Nick."

I scoffed. "I can only imagine his life would be improved without that troll around."

"They've been friends since middle school. Nick's his best friend."

I wanted to ditch. I'd be willing to pose for pictures all afternoon if it meant I didn't have to sit on that stage any longer and listen to questions I didn't understand.

"You know a lot about this show," I finally said to Gretchen.

"Yeah, I studied with Todd for this."

"Todd studied for this?"

"Like I said, he likes to support his friends."

I stifled a groan.

Truth is, if I had my powers, I could go find a universe where something similar to what happened on Galaxy Gang exists. That was the beauty of infinity. Everything is happening everywhere.

I could live among their crew, get promoted to lieutenant or captain or admiral. Go on crazy adventures, dodge bureaucratic responsibilities, and make some questionably effective treaties just like these characters.

I could jump forward in that timeline a thousand years, two thousand maybe, and all those people I served with would be dead and dust. Their actions caused tiny ripples that'd settled into a great lake.

Yet even those ripples wouldn't affect anything outside their universe. Their actions and life were inconsequential. Because of that a cheap retelling of their story here in the form of a network television show was even less impactful to me.

But of course, I couldn't say that to Gretchen. It'd remind her that she was here with some stranger instead of her boyfriend. So I told her another truth.

"Todd wants you to buzz in sooner," I said. It wasn't untruthful. I was Todd; I wanted her to buzz in sooner. Partially because I knew it'd frustrate Nick but also I knew she had the answers.

"You've correctly answered every question," I continued. "Even the ones that bounced back to us after Nick fumbled it to the other team. Todd can't help his friend but you can. You just don't have the arrogance of Nick, which is probably why Todd followed you to college rather than attending whichever community college he's at."

"If we lose this Nick's going to be gloomy all day. And the guys we're up against next are actually good. Semi-finals are where we normally get knocked out."

"If he's upset about a little tournament he's missed the point. Sometimes it helps to have some perspective on the universe."

She scowled at me taking her comment out of context.

I shrugged. "Every Gretchen I've known has enjoyed winning. You're different than most, but I assume you've still got that?"

"Sure," she said. "Todd'd just be bummed if we won without him."

"Nah," I said. "He'd be glad you helped his friend out."

***

We sat under the hot lights. My Traktar mask sat at the edge of the table facing down our opposing team. The last team to beat until we were crowned champions.

My advice to buzz in sooner had worked. The entire semi-final round became a competition between Nick and Gretchen rather than against the other team. Both of them eager to buzz in before the other.

That round ended after only six questions. The only point we gave up was because Justin buzzed in early and flubbed the answer giving the opportunity to the other team. I couldn't begrudge the guy though.

I was glad to see everyone excited. They may not be my friends but some part of Todd from Gretchen's view might've rubbed off on me. Even if tensions were a little high between Nick and me after the round. He couldn't complain about success, at least not without some effort.

I leaned over my buzzer, wanting our team to at least appear as intimidating as possible to the opposing team. Nick had all but given up on expecting me to buzz in. And my performance certainly wasn't for the small crowd, less than a dozen people, that sat dispersed through the auditorium. It'd do everyone a favor to dim the house lights to obscure the pitiful attendance. But I could see all the empty seats before us.

My fingers rested on the big red button feeling the smooth plastic. I'd never press it but my fingers longed to. They itched to participate and I couldn't blame them.

Tides were finally turning in our favor at this point in this final round. Our recent streak of four correct answers in a row was a boon, I just worried it was a little too late.

At the start of this round, the competition between Nick and Gretchen to buzz in first had intensified. Because of this Nick and Gretchen had both given a point to the other team by buzzing in early and answering incorrectly. Nick had done it twice, and I'd be willing to bet it was because he couldn't stand Gretchen buzzing in before him.

Those mistakes, combined with the one time the opposing actually beat us on the buzzer, put us at the final question tied four to four. Whoever answered this question would win the tournament.

The announcer began his question. I had no gauge on whether or not the questions were becoming more difficult. However, considering this question opened by mentioning an alternative timeline arc from season three, I suspected they were.

"...Dr. Erikson used an antidote to cure Captain Kade's Aquolian slug bite. What did she use as the main ingre—"

I expected the silence to be followed by the metallic buzz of a team member chiming in. I hoped it was my own.

Instead, there was only silence.

The edges of my vision went fuzzy with gray static.

A void figure stood across the table from me. It looked down at me, making me feel as if I was a morsel for its dinner. The figure was tall, its waist was half a foot above the table.

Despite its height, the disproportionately long arms ended just above the tabletop. The ends of its arms were fingerless. They drew into a single point instead of a fingered hand. The dark humanoid held me still. My chest was frozen tight. My heart felt like it was racing.

The bright stage lights did little to illuminate more than the outline of the figure. A gateway to emptiness stood in front of me in the shape of a lanky person.

Its head slowly turned to Gretchen who sat next to me. It moved in front of her. Not with a step or a slide, but like the flicker of a screen. None of its appendages seemed necessary for the movement.

Static clouded the edges of my vision so I couldn't see Gretchen's reaction from the corner of my eye. I could see the audience though, the figure no longer blocking my view.

The tournament was suddenly very popular. Every seat was filled.

Void figures were in attendance occupying every empty seat in the auditorium. And there was no shortage of empty seats.

The crowd stood with a flicker.

Static connected from the edges of my vision like a bolt of lightning.

I expected the crowd to fold into the single void figure in front of Gretchen. Just like they had each time before.

Instead, they turned into something more horrifying.

The audience, with the exception of the half dozen convention visitors, were all brunette teenage girls. Some had puffed-up faces, blue from suffocation. Others were mangled with limbs hanging loose from their body, black tread marks covering their skin and clothes. They wore everything from pajamas to gymnastics leotards to regular street clothes.

An army of dead Gretchens stood before me. In a slow plodding march, they approached me. Their broken limbs were merely a minor hindrance to reaching me on the stage.

I looked at the void figure that stood in front of Gretchen. As if the void figure was a doorway a high school-aged Gretchen walked through and occupied the exact place the figure once stood. She wore jeans and a light spring jacket that hung over her crooked collarbone. Each of her shoulders looked like someone hammered them towards the ground.

Her face was mangled by a black eye, scrapes, and cuts exposing bone. Her skull seemed caved in by a rectangular object. She looked down at the Gretchen next to me and lifted her arm.

The limb was jagged broken in multiple places and rose like it was lifted with puppet strings. But it was clear where it was headed.

The crowd of Gretchens had reached the stage and clamored to climb onto it. I didn't know what would happen if they closed in or found the stairs and I didn't want to find out.

The crushed figure in front of Gretchen lifted their arm towards me. With an unbroken hand, despite the state of the rest of her body, a single finger pointed at me. A shattered gold watch hung limply on the wrist.

The figure vanished.

Gretchen let out a scream.

I tried to relax, glad to be free from clamoring ghouls. Something still wasn't quite right.

My fingers pressed down the buzzer.

The announcer looked from Gretchen to me. He gave me a surprised look, likely trying to understand the horror painted on my face, then raised his eyebrows as if to elicit a response.

My mouth didn't feel like my own. The voice that came out merely sounded like mine. The words were not of my choosing. I still felt as frozen as when the void figures stood in front of me.

The trivia answer felt like vomit lurching up my throat. "Culinary Officer Drekzeot's leftover Altairian custard," I answered.

"Correct!" The announcer replied.

I gagged and coughed. Thankfully under my own will.

Nick let out a whoop. Justin and Julia cheered from the far end of the table.

I looked over to Gretchen. Finally able to get a good look at her.

She looked back at me for only a moment. Her green nose and forehead crinkled in revulsion.

7

We didn't stay much longer after the tournament. Nick enjoyed getting to carry the trophy around the convention room floor. We posed for a few more pictures but Gretchen was in a sour mood and it seemed everyone could tell, except Nick.

Gretchen barely said anything to me on the way home. She asked for no explanation about the countless mangled versions of herself that filled the auditorium. Not that I had much of one.

When I joked that she should've just left me there at the convention to find my own way home since she was so upset she flatly responded that she wanted to make sure Todd's body made it home in one piece.

And she did.

She dropped me off at the stairway of Todd's apartment building. Did everything except walk me to the door. And I didn't hear her drive away until the front door shut behind me.

I was exhausted from the day grateful to make it to the bedroom. I set the mask down on the desk. I removed some of the bulkier foam armor that would keep me from sleeping. Then laid back on the bed. My legs ached from walking around all day.

Which is why it was unsurprising that I quickly fell into a dreamless sleep.

What was surprising was waking up in just gym shorts in a different bed.

It was still night, only the orange glow of street lights peak in from the window across from the bed. The bed smelled different, like floral laundry detergent. The comforter had paisley swirls on it, purple and yellow, which matched most of the decor of the room.

The room was a mirrored version of the default Todd's room. The desk was where the bed used to be. And it was cluttered with binders and books instead of miniature figurines.

Something clattered to the ground in the other room. The door was closed so it muffled the quiet curses that followed but I could still make it out as Gretchen's voice.

I rolled across the bed since the side I was sleeping on was against the wall. The half of the bed that Gretchen recently laid in was still warm. I found a shirt that fit me in the pile of clothes on the ground and pulled it on.

Something crinkled in the pocket of my shorts.

I pulled out a piece of paper folded in half so it barely fit in the large pocket of the shorts. I unfolded it and in neat square handwriting, there was a note addressed to me.

Todd Prime,

Gretchen has been making sure I got to bed at a reasonable hour for the past month but I hope tonight I will have kept myself up long enough to exhaust myself and let you out. Or summon you. I don't know how any of this works.

What I do know is that Gretchen needs help. Keeping myself up late was easy since she's barely been sleeping lately. She's having nightmares, and won't talk to anyone about it, but she wakes up in the night screaming and shuttering. She won't go to a doctor for it, not that I suspect they'll be able to help.

Who knows if you'll even be able to do anything? But I figured it was worth a shot. From what Gretchen tells me you don't care about anything much more than yourself. But maybe you care about her and she just has a hard time understanding.

Anyway, congrats on winning the tournament, bummed I wasn't there to see it. After finals are over next week we can spend some time getting you out of my body. I'm sure we'd both appreciate that.

Peace & Prosper,

Just Todd

I folded the note back up tightly so it didn't take up my whole pocket. I took a deep breath to prepare myself for whatever I was about to walk into with Gretchen.

I tried to latch onto a universe, mostly out of habit, but nothing caught. What I wouldn't do to get out of here. But this was what I came for, seeing a Gretchen that had nightmares to the point of being unable to sleep.

I just wish it didn't have to be this Gretchen.

I walked out the bedroom door, shutting it gently behind me. The main living area of the apartment was similar to default Todd's apartment, just mirrored. Mirroring a floor plan probably saved the designers time. Plus, college kids didn't care if their apartment was unique, they were just glad not to be living with their parents.

The bedroom door opened to a small dining room with a table covered in bags and books. One of the bags was Gretchen's brown leather bag still splotched with light red.

Across from the dining room was the kitchen where Gretchen stood over a cutting board. Harsh fluorescent lights shone down on her and cast long shadows across everything else in the dark apartment.

The living room was a little messier than Todd's with dirty plates and aluminum cans littered across the various side tables. It was too dark to make out the details of the mess but it was unlike the Gretchens I knew to leave a mess. So either the trash belonged to her roommate, or this Gretchen was not acting like the others. Based on my experience with this Gretchen I had a hunch which it was.

Unlike Todd's apartment, the walls had no movie posters hanging on them. They were bare with the exception of a large TV mounted to the wall next to the roommate's closed door. The floor-to-ceiling vertical blinds were cracked open letting a bit of light in from the balcony.

"Hey. Sorry. Did I wake you?" Gretchen asked. She held a large chef knife in one hand and a peeled carrot in the other.

Her hair was pulled back in a ponytail. Tight bike shorts peeked out from under an oversized shirt.

She was dressed somewhere between about to go for a run and just rolled out of bed. I suspected the shirt belonged to default Todd because multiple superhero faces were printed on it in a grid.

"It's fine," I said. "What are you making?" I walked across the dining room and leaned against the counter. A large stock pot was filled with diced onions and celery and it sat next to a rotisserie chicken still sitting in its plastic clamshell container.

Gretchen looked at me skeptically and then sliced the carrot in half lengthwise. "My mom's rotisserie chicken noodle soup. Couldn't sleep so I figured I'd work on some lunch."

I looked at the clock on the oven. "It's 3 AM. Lunch isn't for a while."

She hacked into the carrot with heavy strokes and each cut made a snapping sound that seemed to echo through the apartment.

"You're not worried about your roommate?" I said pointing to the kitchen wall that was shared with the second bedroom.

Gretchen scraped up the diced carrots onto her knife the dumped them into the pot banging the spine of the knife loudly on the rim to knock the few straggling bits of carrot off. She kept at it after they all fell off. The sound was uncomfortable this late at night.

"What are you doing here?" She pointed the tip of the knife at me. It was the first good look I'd gotten at her face in a while. It wasn't painted green. She didn't have any other makeup on either. But the purple bags under her eyes would be hard to hide even if she did.

The whites of her eyes had small red veins reaching towards her hazel irises. Her nose wrinkled in disgust as if the chicken on the counter had spoiled. But the knife in my face made it clear her disgust was directed at me.

"I came from the bedroom... where we were sleeping." I smiled nonchalantly. "That is until you decided to make an early lunch."

"I'm too tired to play games, Todd." She put the knife down and opened the clamshell container of the rotisserie chicken. She pulled the well-seasoned brown skin off the bird and dropped it into the container's lid like it was a used tissue. Then she tore into the meat of the breast shredding it to tiny chunks before adding it to the pot.

"I'm not—"

"My Todd knows Marissa stays with her boyfriend on weekends. My Todd knew I was going to cook this soup because he went to the grocery store for me. My Todd doesn't look at me like I'm some stray dog that needs a home."

"Didn't want to break your immersion," I said with a shrug. "That's what you wanted at the convention."

"Break my immersion?" Gretchen let out a weak chuckle. "You know what breaks my immersion? Not being able to sleep because of my constant nightmares. You know what's giving me these night-mares?"

"I could wager a guess."

"I bet you could." She pulled a drumstick off the bird, stripped its skin, and then broke the meat of the drumstick off dropping it straight into the pot. "What I can't even remotely guess at is why you'd do it?"

Gretchen grabbed the knife covering its black handle with grease from the chicken.

She cut into the leg joint of the bird trying to separate the thigh from the body. The knife wasn't particularly sharp so she employed a sawing motion towards herself to get through the skin. She broke through after a moment. It was no small of effort.

"I didn't give you the nightmares," I protested.

The knife was too wide to get to the tendons easily. She probed around the meat with the back of the knife. I would've used the tip but I kept my mouth shut. She didn't seem particularly open to my advice.

"You gave them to me like humidity gives me frizzy hair. Nothing I can do about it. It's just going to happen to me anyway."

She found what she was looking for and restarted her sawing mo-tion. Her nose and eyebrows wrinkled in frustration. She wrenched the thigh in the opposite way it was meant to bend. That didn't help so she invested more power into the cutting.

The knife slipped out of the bird.

She had enough force behind the motion that it cut through the tender skin of her palm without a problem.

Gretchen cursed in pain.

She clutched her hands together. The knife fell to the ground miss-ing her bare feet. It clattered against the tile.

The bird made an escape from the packaging but didn't go much further than the cutting board.

Gretchen covered the flesh of her palm with her other hand pressing on it in pain. It seemed to have cut her on the big muscle of her thumb. She bit her lip and closed her eyes with a wince.

I found a roll of paper towels sitting on the counter behind her. It sat in a wire holder next to a knife block of a half dozen other knives and a glass blender. I ripped a sheet off got it wet under the sink and pressed it into her clasped hands.

She took it with her uninjured hand then scowled at me as if I'd cut her myself.

"Sorry," I said unable to come up with anything helpful.

She took my place at the sink running cold water over her palm.

"You need anything?" I asked. "First aid kit or something?"

"I have bandages in my room. I can get one myself."

"Is it bad?" I asked

She walked off into the bedroom without an answer.

I picked up the knife from the floor and placed it in the sink. Then I turned to the counter behind me to find the right knife for the job.

After a few guesses, all the plastic black handles looked the same, I found the thin-bladed knife made for carving meat. I tested the edge to see what I was working with. It was sharp enough, likely only due to neglect. I found a honing rod, obvious with its round handle, and swiped the blade against it. It wouldn't sharpen the knife but I was willing to take any help I could get.

Reorienting the chicken on the cutting board I found the thigh joint and sliced through the tendons. I took off the other leg, still whole with the drumstick attached.

Animals were easy to butcher, regardless of their species or their planet of origin. I'd done it countless times across countless lives. It was second nature.

Evolution did most of the work for me already. I just had to find a joint, which was always the weakest part of the animal, and separate the bones there.

I separated the wings from the upper portion of the carcass. Once the final appendage was removed I dropped the ribcage into the plastic container. it was picked clean from Gretchen's previous work.

Gretchen returned as I started slicing the bones out of the thighs. She took a seat at the bar and looked down at the workstation I was at.

"Why'd you do it?" She asked.

"Didn't think you'd be able to cook much more of the chicken with your hand like that." I cut through the tip of the wing, discarded it in the container then started cutting the boneless meat into smaller pieces.

"You're gonna make me say it?" Gretchen groaned. "Something's wrong in your head."

"I killed you because I had to."

"Had to?" Gretchen said with a scoff.

"I was investigating your death. I had to watch you die countless times. Once I figured out I was behind the murders I had to follow through with my own actions. But all those deaths made me appreciate the Gretchen I saved. I died for her."

"You died once for her and were resurrected afterward. She—I died, countless times.

"Painfully, I might add. Do you know what it feels like to have your throat close up against your will? To suffocate to death?"

"Do you?" I looked up at her and raised my eyebrows. She wasn't those Gretchens. She hadn't actually died. I hoped she wouldn't for a long time.

"Based on my dreams... yeah. I have a pretty good idea. It's excruciatingly slow. Every moment's filled with terror. There's no pain. Just a lack of air, as if I can't grasp onto the one thing I need."

She shivered in reaction to the memory. "But sure your one death is noble." She didn't sound convinced.

"I'd lived so many lives I can't remember them all at that point. I wasn't confident I'd live, at least the version of myself that was under the car. When I finally ran myself over to complete the cycle I knew it'd unlock more power and was necessary. But at the time death, true death, an extinguishing of my consciousness, could've destroyed so much."

"But a bunch of teenage Gretchens. Those deaths meant nothing. Hell our lives, our potential futures, were no more meaningful than this chicken." She pointed at the picked-apart carcass in the plastic container.

"Effectively, yes."

Gretchen roared in frustration and banged her hands against the counter. She then cursed hurting her recently cut hand and pressed the bandage down to soothe herself.

"Think about it. There are infinite universes. Every time a decision is made the universe splits. Todd bought this chicken, but there are countless other universes where Todd picked other chickens or you decided to cook chili instead of chicken soup.

"And then there are the universes that are insignificantly different because someone else made a decision that doesn't affect us. There are more of you throughout the multiverse than there are dead chickens on this planet. I'm sorry. You're just not significant."

I scraped the last of the chicken off the cutting board and straight into the pot. I looked across the bar at Gretchen. She was staring solemnly at the meat I'd just added to the pot.

"I'm sorry," I said. I tried to be as genuine as I could. Unlike butchering, I didn't have years of experience doing that.

"No. I know you're right. That's the worst part."

"Hey, sometimes I'm wrong about things."

"Not this. I know I'm insignificant. Not in a learn-it-in-a-book kind of way but in the way I know how to drive a car. It's inside me, understood, felt."

Gretchen shivered.

"I can feel my insignificance with every dream I have. The death and dying, it sucks. But I could get through the nightmares, dismiss them if I had to.

"I can feel the universe closing in around me after I die. I can feel my mind being shrunk to the size of a grain of sand. Insignificantly floating in the ocean and that ocean is just on a planet that's insignificant compared to the galaxy or cosmos or multiverse."

Gretchen looked up at me. "I've felt it so many times I can't reject it."

"What needs to be done next?" I looked at the pot.

"Todd. I'm not supposed to know this. I'm not supposed to have this perspective. It should feel abstract to me. But my insignificance is as concrete to me as this counter. And I can't keep living like this."

"I seem to manage." I found the recipe under the stockpot. It was written on a piece of notebook paper in Gretchen's curvy handwriting. I skimmed for the next step.

"You don't have an option. You literally tried to kill yourself and didn't die. Me, I have a way out."

I put down the recipe and looked up at her. I needed to add chicken broth and didn't know where it was. Didn't seem like the time to ask. Instead, I asked, "You know why I came here?"

"It sure wasn't to win a trivia tournament."

"Gretchens are killing themselves across the multiverse. I've visited two. From what I know about the multiverse I'd bet there are countless more.

"They're all having nightmares like you. They're all probably having the same perspective problem you are. I found you to try and stop it. Except I can't."

I stepped back to lean on the counter behind me. The food was at an impasse. Just like my pursuit of helping Gretchen.

Gretchen chuckled. "All because you decided to kill me just so you could have someone precious to you."

"Don't kill yourself," I stated flatly. "It's not the solution, and I don't want to see any more dead Gretchens."

"Sure feels like a solution."

From the deep recesses of my memory, I pulled out what Gretchen had told me when I came to her with a similar problem.

"At the very least live your short life, here with this Todd that you seem to love. After all, what's another 90 years compared to 90 minutes in the grand scheme of things?"

Gretchen scoffed and it grew to a legitimate laugh. It sounded like a bell and was a nice change of tone. "As much as I appreciate the logic, and your optimism that medical technology with improve human lifespans so significantly, right now my mind is not firing on logic. Hell, it doesn't feel like it's even my own."

"How so?" I asked.

"I don't want to die. But just like how I don't want to cry in a sad movie my emotions drag me that way anyway. It's this invasive thought that keeps elbowing its way into my inner dialogue, telling me it'd be easier if I wasn't having to wade through this bullshit.

"I can ignore it in class, or during volleyball practice. But at 3 AM, after a nightmare or two, cooking soup does little to assuage me. And I only have so much energy to fight it. Eventually, I'll lose. Maybe not this week, or month, or year. But it'll get me eventually. Just like you got me in every universe. Taking my breath away in the least romantic way possible."

"How real are those dreams to you?" I asked. I pushed myself away from the counter. Her comment about breath gave me an idea.

"As if I was there living them myself." Her tone was desperate and full of sorrow.

"Let's try an exercise in breathing," I suggested.

"I need medication more than I need meditation."

I flipped the light for the kitchen off. The room was dark except for the orange street lights coming in from the balcony.

Gretchen swiveled her bar chair following me with her eyes as I went into the living room. I pulled a few cushions off the couch, they came away with the loud rip of separating velcro. I placed them on the ground then took a seat on one.

"There's not a prescription drug in the world that can beat this." I patted the cushion across from me inviting Gretchen to join.

"And non-prescription drugs?" Gretchen asked climbing down from the barstool like a dog being lured out of a kennel.

"If you've got any, I doubt they'd hurt the process?" I said with a smile.

Gretchen squatted down to the cushion and sat cross-legged. Her big superhero T-shirt covered her knees. Only her toes poked out from the edges each nail painted white at the tips.

"Sorry I'm fresh out," she answered. The smile on her face barely cut through the sorrow in her eyes. But the fact it cut through gave me hope this might work.

8

I regretted my decision almost immediately. Three hours later, with the early morning sun peaking through the balcony window my regret was well justified.

Gretchen sat across from me, a fuzzy brown blanket draped over her shoulders. Her breathing was heavy like she'd just run a mile or three. She always did this right before—

"UGH I can't do it," Gretchen complained.

We looked like we were having a seance. Hell, having a seance might've been easier.

Scented candles of various colors filled the air with a medley of smells. Depending where you pointed your nose you could get anything from Christmas spices to a fresh ocean breeze. We even dragged out a bacon-scented one that Gretchen got as a gag gift at a postseason volleyball gift exchange.

The candles were supposed to be calming. Gretchen was so tired very little seemed to calm her right now.

"Just breathe evenly. Deep breaths. But not forced breaths. You'll feel something in your mind."

"I feel a headache in my mind." Gretchen shrugged off the blanket. I knew she'd drape it back over her shoulders soon. Not because it was particularly cold in the apartment. It was just something for her to do in protest of the exercise.

And exercise was a generous description of what I was having Gretchen do. I was no great teacher like Admiral Betrix, Master Kan Chai, or Gandalf. I knew this because Gretchen told me, repeatedly, with far more names than I remembered or recognized.

Despite that, neither of us gave up. If only to avoid showing weakness to the other.

"Can we try something different?" I asked.

"You have another method of traveling the multiverse?" Gretchen said, her tone seethed with sarcasm. "Shoulda brought that up hours ago."

I scooted my cushion towards her so my knees were a hair away from hers. The cushions, upholstered in vinyl and filled with cheap foam stuffing, were flattened to the ground. Much like me, it was not doing great at its job.

I placed my hands on my knees. My fingers stretched just over the gap between our legs. "Hold my hands?" I felt stupid asking. I had no idea what holding hands was going to do.

Gretchen frowned at me in confusion. But she didn't protest. She rested her hands in mine. We clasped our fingers around each other's palms.

The bandage on her left palm felt rough in my right hand. The rest of her skin was smooth and warm.

I missed her touch and smiled at the comfort it brought me. I wondered if anything I did for her was comforting. From her view, she was sitting across from a stranger, a monster even. Someone who'd brought only chaos into her life.

I closed my eyes and took a deep breath. As if I was going to travel. As if I was going to escape the consequences of my actions yet again.

I heard Gretchen follow my lead and take a similarly deep breath.

"Feel out with your mind to find a world you want to go to." I took my advice and went through the steps I explained with my mind.

Gretchen responded with a huff. It wasn't unjustified. I'd used that explanation a dozen times.

I took a few breaths to center myself and more importantly think of a better explanation.

"Don't reach for anything. Imagine yourself in the universe you want to be in. Imagine a place, similar to somewhere you've been. Maybe a gymnasium or a friend's house or a restaurant that serves your favorite food. Even if it doesn't exist here, it exists somewhere in the multiverse."

I took a few breaths letting Gretchen think about a place she wanted to be. Likely anywhere would be better than here, or at least with me.

I wondered, as I waited if this was how I learned the first time. Or if I just appeared one day in a different universe after taking a deep breath. I'd been doing it for so long that it was second nature. I rarely spent more than a half dozen decades in any given universe.

Gretchen's breath was relaxed. I continued on. "Imagine you're walking through the place. Pick up objects, interact with people. What smells are in the air? What sounds echo through the room?"

Gretchen's fingers twitched in my palms. Her breaths were measured, unwavering. An improvement over previous attempts.

Then she let go of my hands.

Disappointed by the sudden abandonment I opened my eyes.

Gretchen was no longer sitting in front of me.

The immediate excitement at our success, her success, quickly evaporated when I realized I hadn't taught her how to get back.

Gretchen disappeared into the multiverse and I had no way to find her. Something in the back of my mind roared in frustration. It wasn't a vocalized scream like hearing Gretchen across the multiverse. Instead, it was a muted berating and self-doubt, something I rarely experienced.

I stood up and started pacing around the room. For no particular reason, I picked between my teeth. Default Todd's short nails did little to get in between the gaps of our teeth but scratching scum off the enamel was still comforting.

After a few short laps around the small apartment, I kicked the cushion I had squished flat. It puffed up. I sat on it and it instantly deflated under my weight.

I started taking deep breaths. I had to be able to travel again. If the void figures were deities that took away my powers then surely teaching Gretchen this amazing skill would be penance enough.

Or they were demons hell-bent on punishing me.

Religion and fantasy were never the right way to explain misunderstood phenomena. Clearly, I wasn't thinking straight.

My mind was racing too fast to latch onto anything. I'd have to be focused to find this particular Gretchen in the sea of the multiverse.

"Am I back?" Gretchen asked from the kitchen.

I opened my eyes and turned my head. Gretchen stood in front of the stockpot. The bar height counter blocked all but her head from my vantage point on the floor.

"You're back!" I said.

"Good! You've been confused by that comment in the past five universes I went to."

"You went to five universes?" I asked. "How long have you been gone?" She could have lived ten lifetimes before returning to me. A hundred even. Then chosen to appear merely minutes after her first appearance.

Assuming she remembered where this universe was located after that much time. I certainly couldn't remember my original universe anymore.

"Shouldn't I be asking you that?"

"It's been five or six minutes. I was worried sick."

"Good!" Gretchen smiled walked out of the kitchen and picked her cushion up off the floor. "Although I can't imagine why. I suspect I'm as immortal as you." She placed the cushion on the couch and after some finagling with the velcro, she aligned it the way she wanted it. She reached her bandaged hand out to me to help me off the ground.

I placed my right hand in hers. She began to pull me up as she said, "I shouldn't need to sit on the ground—"

The apartment began to shake. The flames of the candles waved slowly in the air. Nothing fell from the counters or shelves. The TV that hung behind Gretchen kept its place despite the shake being strong enough to knock it off of whatever bolts held it up.

Unsurprisingly Gretchen had two void figures flanking her. The expectation of their appearance didn't make it comfortable. They looked down at me, still seated on the floor clasping Gretchen's hand in the shape of a clam.

Gray static, like being tuned into the wrong channel on an old TV, inched in on the edge of my vision.

The flat-screen TV behind Gretchen showed me a reflection of the rest of the living room, thanks to the black surface catching the bright morning sunlight.

The room appeared as expected. A couch, a white wall, a pile of messy plates on the side table. The only exceptional part of the image was the dozen black humanoid shapes. They spotted the reflection like lanky human shapes that punched through reality.

The figures reached their arms out for Gretchen's. She was busy staring at the group behind me, unable to turn her head to observe behind her. I could watch just fine.

And what I saw terrified me.

Handless arms reached for Gretchen's forearm. It was difficult to tell if they ever connected since their bodies merely appeared as a gap in reality.

Once the figure on the left grabbed Gretchen's forearm she could see what it was doing. She watched the void figure cover her arm with theirs. It seemed to blot out her arm's existence.

Her eyes darted away. She was unable to employ her nose or eyebrows in the process of wincing at the experience. I continued to watch in horror, unable to turn my head away, as the figure's limb extended and twisted up Gretchen's arm like a vine spiraling up a trellis. The bizarre movement could only be done with a boneless arm.

I looked at Gretchen's eyes. She stared back at me. Eyes panicked.

The gray static at the edge of my vision was growing towards the center. I knew it'd connect soon. The figures would collapse into one being, then they'd disappear once again.

I couldn't hold Gretchen's hand any tighter. My muscles were frozen. Only my brain and internal organs seemed to work. They made up for my paralysis by racing at double speed.

The static connected from the edge of my vision.

It grew out, covering my entire field of view.

I was blinded by gray and white and black lines of static. My blindness heightened my other senses.

I could smell each variety of scented candles. I could feel the thin cushion and hard floor under my butt. I could hear the dull hum of the apartment's AC.

Those sensations disappeared as well.

If I hadn't already died under an SUV, I would've assumed this was death.

My feet dangled under me like I was falling through the air. No cushion supported me. I could kick my feet, my muscles were back under my control. Although they did me little good.

My stomach crawled up my throat like I was falling but no wind whipped past my head. No matter where I turned my head I saw static, adding to my disorientation.

The only thing I could sense in this staticky vacuum was Gretchen's hand. The soft warm flesh of her palm was growing clammy everywhere except the rough bandage over the muscle near her thumb.

I clasped her hand tight. I didn't want the only thing I had in this void to slip out of my grasp.

She gripped me back. I pulled her towards me. Her body emerged from the static, like an anchor lifted out of the ocean.

I reached for her body. Her oversized superhero shirt billowed around her like a Victorian dress, despite the windlessness of our fall. I clutched the fabric tight against her body as I wrapped my arm around her waist.

She threw her right arm around my neck and across my upper back. She hooked onto the far edge of my shoulder blade near my armpit.

Like a clam protecting itself from a threat, we tighten the grip of our hands. Neither of us was willing to reposition them for fear of losing grip on the other.

In gym clothes and loungewear, we fell through the void like tango dancers.

9

"That answers what happens when you walk all the way down the west corridor," Gretchen said as she emerged from the hallway we'd labeled as the east wing.

The room we were trapped in had archaic vaulted ceilings with mosaic tile work showing detailed pictures of nebulas and galaxies. It would've taken centuries to do it by hand. And it didn't make sense that something so old would have images that were so modern, even futuristic depending where you stood in time.

Rows of bookshelves spanned out in every direction. The books on them were bound in either leather, plastic, cheap paper, or materials I was unfamiliar with. Most of them were unreadable to me, either a language I recognized but didn't speak or unrecognizable symbols I could only imagine the meaning of.

A pile of books I could read, along with my leather trench coat, sat next to me on a table. The table was one of many in the center of the room. Bookshelf hallways radiated out in every direction.

The table I sat on was near the eastern edge where I expected Gretchen to come out. There were sixteen tables in total, placed neatly in a square. The table was sturdy, made of hardwood I couldn't identify. The whole room smelled like a sawmill as if the wood that filled it had just been cut by hand. The top was planed smooth while the legs were intricately carved with leaves blooming into flowers that held the tabletop in place.

My feet rested on the wooden chair in front of me. Its ornately carved back depicted a fish leaping out of water. The artwork was uncomfortable to lean against, hence why I sat on the table.

I kicked the chair over in frustration. It knocked against the chair behind it. That chair was carved just as ornately: a large bug-eyed animal with an insect-like exoskeleton hanging from a tree limb like a sloth. The wooden clanking sound echoed through the cavernous roof.

Gretchen had set out to walk down the west wing to see if it came to an end or exit. Just like the northern wing I'd walked down a while ago, she exited on the opposite side of the room.

If her experience was like mine, and I had no reason to doubt it was, she would've walked straight down the hallway, books towering over her, without ever taking a turn. The towering bookshelves made the walk dim but never pitch black. Eventually, a light would appear at the end of the bookshelf tunnel. Unfortunately in both cases that light turned out to be the grid of tables we'd landed on after falling out of the static gray void.

I jumped off the table. My boots thunked on the tiled floor. The tiles were an opaque turquoise stone with spirals of orange crystals interlaced in the rock like a type of granite I'd never seen before. I was in my traveling outfit, jeans, and a black T-shirt. My familiar body with a few days of facial hair, unkempt hair, and just enough aches to remind me I was no longer in the body of a twenty-year-old college kid.

Gretchen hadn't changed a bit. She still wore bike shorts and her default Todd's oversized superhero t-shirt. Her bare feet made a light pitter-patter on the tiled floor.

She never asked why I looked different. Probably recognized me from her dreams. It was the most logical reason why she'd avoided eye contact since arrival.

"Which means we're trapped," Gretchen concluded. "I learn how to travel the multiverse and immediately get whisked away to some multi-dimensional prison."

"What happened after you left the apartment?" I asked leaning against a table. It was sturdy enough that it didn't slide out from under me.

Gretchen shrugged and took a seat in one of the wooden chairs. She grimaced as she shifted her back trying to find a comfortable position. After a moment she gave up and leaned forward. "I wound up in a gymnasium. It was kind of like the one at our high school if you remember it."

I didn't but nodded my head as if I did.

"The layout was a bit different. Risers were on the opposite side, school colors were maroon and white instead of blue and white. The coach was different too and I didn't recognize most of my teammates.

"I appeared in the universe midair between the uneven bars. I must've been in the middle of practicing a routine. Fell straight into the pads. I'm surprised I didn't hurt anything."

"You were in the body of a default Gretchen?" I asked.

"Don't call her that," she scolded but didn't suggest anything better. "I was though. Felt strange... surreal even. I didn't know any of my teammate's names, or my routine. I let someone else take a go and got some water. Then tried to breathe like you told me to return to my apartment."

"Which I guess worked."

"After a few tries. There's a lot of Todds like mine. Most of them were very confused when their Gretchen asked if she was back. Although all of the Gretchens I wound up possessing were standing in their kitchen before a stockpot in the middle of the night. Made it easy for me to find my way home."

"That doesn't bode well for those Gretchens," I said.

"I didn't have their memories. But I could feel their uneasiness. It was like their bodies influenced my mind." Gretchen shivered. The room wasn't particularly cold. "They were exhausted in the same way I was earlier in the night."

"Hmmm," I said.

"And I don't know how to save them. They're going to kill themselves."

I offered Gretchen my jacket off the table knocking over the stack of books it sat next to.

She looked up at me then away wrinkling her nose at the jacket. "What am I supposed to do?"

"We don't have to do anything?" I threw the jacked over the chair next to her then paced down the grid of tables. "Can't do much of anything here."

"I have to do something? Hell, you should do something. You're the one who made this mess."

"What do you want me to do? I can't even travel."

Neither of us could, it was the first thing we tried when we landed on the tables here.

"I'm traumatized. All of the Gretchens are. Don't you feel any remorse for that?"

"Of course I do," I immediately replied.

Gretchen stared me down. The first time she'd genuinely looked me in the eye since we arrived. As uncomfortable as it was for me I'm sure it was harder for her.

"I'm sorry that you're hurting. I thought teaching you to travel would help. But how am I supposed to feel bad for every suicidal Gretchen in the multiverse? I didn't have a choice, it was how my life was supposed to go. Things get weird when you try to mess up your own past."

Gretchen groaned and looked past me at the rows of bookshelves that disappeared in the distance behind me. "Well, we can't just let them suffer... at least I can't."

"If you've got a way to help I'm—"

The sound of wood splitting cut me off. We both looked to my left and a bi-pedal owl walked out of the side of a bookcase and into the room.

He had brown feathers that covered his body. He wore a purple robe draped across his chest like a sash, it seemed to be weighed down in spots making me suspect it had pockets.

His face had large yellow-orange eyes with eyebrows that swooped away from the center like a soaring bird. His wings hunched over him like two guards, dark brown at the top fading to long white feathers towards the bottom edge.

The bookcase had no doorway that he walked through. Instead, it appeared, if only for a second, that he'd walked in from a hallway I didn't see. But by the time I'd taken the whole situation in he was merely standing in the room next to Gretchen and me.

"Thank you for your patience," the owl said cordially. "Your orientation is to begin shortly. Follow me." He looked at Gretchen as he spoke. His voice had a hollow sound to it as if each word took twice as much air to puff out.

Unlike a normal bird, this owl-man had arms covered in small brown feathers that went all the way past his wrist like a long-sleeved shirt. His torso looked more like a griffin or an angel than an actual bird.

The end of his arm had a leathery hand with four talons protruding from the center. They weren't quite sharp enough to cut anything though. And it was as if the owl got manicures on the weekend to keep his claws at bay. His feet were similar, covered in feathers giving him the appearance of large thighs that went straight to the ankle. Except the talons on his feet were sharp enough that I didn't want to be on the other end of them.

He offered his strange talon hand to Gretchen who sat forward in her chair as perplexed as me.

The owl-man moved his fingers up and down in a gesture that seemed impatient.

"What orientation?" Gretchen asked.

"I'll lead you through it. This way please." He moved his hand closer to Gretchen's which were clutched just past her knees. "You can trust me."

"That's exactly what someone you can't trust would say," I rebutted.

The owl twisted his head like a cap being screwed off a jar and looked at me.

I stumbled back a step, unsettled by the movement.

He hooted in my direction. It was hollow and high-pitched. "Your associate here has a good point," the owl said words still sounding airy. "But I assure you we brought you here for your own safety Mrs. Smith."

"What else are we going to do?" Gretchen asked me. She unclutched her hands and grabbed the owl-man's talon. He helped her stand up out of the chair and led her away from the bank of tables.

From my perspective, they didn't go down a hallway of bookcases. Instead, it seemed, if only for a moment, that they walked around a corner I couldn't see.

I was alone in the expansive library. I flipped through the books. I put my jacket back on, then took it off. I spent minutes, maybe hours, alone. Wandered down numerous hallways of books. I examined the ends of the bookcases, wondering if I could find the hallway the owl-man took Gretchen down. None of it was particularly successful and therefore didn't hold my attention for long.

I tried breathing again trying to travel out of the library. The focused breaths were as useless as they'd been since getting breakfast with Gretchen days ago. Weeks ago even, although I wasn't conscious for most of it.

When Gretchen walked back into the room I was staring up at the mosaic of the nebula trying to calculate how many stones were used. It seemed to be the least impossible task in the room as far as I could tell.

"So, that was interesting," she said interrupting my counting. The number fell out of my memory and I didn't care that I'd lost it.

Gretchen stood in the center of the bank of tables in a purple robe with long sleeves that opened up like a lily at the ends. She was no longer barefoot, instead, she wore thin black flats made of a similar canvas material as the robe. The neckline of her t-shirt poked out between the fold of the robe but the grid of superhero faces was hidden.

"Are you oriented?" I asked dryly.

"Not in the slightest," she rearranged the purple robe trying to get it to lay comfortably without bunching up the shirt underneath. "It's going to take me lifetimes to figure out what's going on here. But apparently, I have that now."

"Lucky us," I replied as I picked up a book. "I haven't found anything particularly interesting in these. The ones I can read are mostly textbooks from throughout time, every other one contradicts the last." I started to flip to a page that I'd dog-eared to show her an example.

"These shelves are full of every book written across every civilization across every universe across all time. Look, Todd, we have a problem."

"Hm. Thought there'd be more then. Was that covered in your orientation?"

"It was. A couple other things were covered as well. Like how you're wanted for crimes against the multiverse."

"Oh." I put the book down. "You brought up the whole killing you in the other universes thing?"

"Yeah, I brought up the you killing me in other universes thing! It's kind of problem number one. Or at least it was."

"What's the new problem number one?" I asked.

"I was tasked with bringing you in," Gretchen said. "We believe your mind has been manipulated, and here we can fix it."

"My mind is fine. It's normal to forget details of your life when you're as long-lived as me," I explained. "And what do you mean you were tasked with bringing me in? A little while ago you didn't even know how to travel."

"Well I specifically didn't have the task, but it was assigned... It'd be easier for her to explain it."

I heard wood cracking as the owl-man walked out from the side of a bookcase followed by a woman who was about the age my current body appeared to be. She was familiar if only because I'd spent a few lifetimes married to her.

10

Gretchen standing next to an older version of herself made the bipedal owl in the room feel like a rounding error of strangeness.

Unlike the owl, or the Gretchen I appeared with, the older Gretchen, older by ten years or ten lifetimes I didn't know, wasn't wearing a purple robe. Instead, she had black jeans and tennis shoes, a short leather coat, also black. There must be something about multiverse traveling and leather jackets, the details of which I'm still fuzzy on. An azure blue t-shirt underneath the jacket added the barest pop of color. Her blonde hair was cut short, nearly reaching her shoulders.

Her face looked marginally less sleep-deprived compared to the Gretchen I arrived with. But it looked twice as stern as if the wrinkled nose and bunched-up eyebrows that Gretchen made when she was disgusted with me had set permanently on her face. The wrinkles that the expression was starting to form were strange to see on the familiar face. I always remembered noticing wrinkles from around the corner of her mouth and eyes first.

On her left wrist, she had a shattered gold watch too big for her arm. It dangled around by her hand. Her opposite wrist had a purple worm wrapped around it. Towards the edges, it was difficult to see where it ended and Gretchen's skin began. It'd leeched itself onto her tighter than the watch had.

Inside of the purple worm, an object glowed gold through the thin skin. The object seemed to be swimming around like a fish in a tank. Like the bipedal owl, cracks in the bookshelves, and endless hallways no one seemed to care or give it a second thought.

I was sick of it.

"It's about time I got my own orientation about this place," I complained.

"You received your orientation ages ago Toodd." the owl person's vowels were long and hollow.

"Well, I don't remember it. So why don't we go over it all again?"

"My name is," the owl person proceeded to make a long hoot followed by a sharp click of his beak, "you call me Woah Te. We are inside the library branch of the Celestial Mother Tree, it seemed the safest place to keep you."

"And the Celestial Mother Tree is...?" Woah Te was giving me more questions than answers.

"A multidimensional being whose branches and roots can fold time and space making new hallways and rooms inside itself." Woah Te gestured to the edge of a bookcase which split with a loud crack and revealed a long wood-paneled hallway. "The Mother used to be able to travel the multiverse, we believe, but now reaches into multiple universes with her roots and branches. She invited us into her branches giving us shelter from time."

"It's also not actually a tree," Gretchen, the one I arrived with, explained. "The avian people just called it that when they discovered it because that description was most similar to the trees their ancestors lived in."

"New travelers of the multiverse always find themselves here," Woah Te said as he started walking down the hallway his sharp talons clicked against the hardwood floor.

Both Gretchens followed.

I grabbed my trench coat, unsure of what leaving it behind in a multidimensional being would do, and followed the trio.

The wooden hallway had long panels of wood arching across the ceiling. A little below waist height band of intricately carved moulding seemed to move like waves in the direction we traveled. It reminded me of lighted paths on space stations to direct passenger movement. Picture frame molding was carved into the wall below the wavy band giving us a sense of moving forward on a hallway that had no visual end.

I hoped that, unlike the hallway of bookcases, this one would end in a different room than we started.

"How do new travelers always find their way here?" I asked Woah Te. My voice echoing off the long hallway.

"We make sure they do," Gretchen, the one in the black jacket, replied. "By grabbing ourselves out of time when we discover our powers. Like I did with Gretchen. You just happened to tag along."

"Which we appreciate," Woah Te hooted almost gleefully. "As we've been trying to track you down for a while now."

"Because of my crimes?" I asked.

"Partially," Woah Te said with more hollowness than normal. He seemed hesitant. "Your actions, against Mrs. Smith are out of the ordinary. Our inability to track you was the first clue that something was wrong."

"I didn't have a choice," I said. "I had to follow my past self I—"

Woah Te cut me off with a loud click. "I am aware of why it was necessary and inevitable from your perspective. As I explained to Mrs.

Smith crime is not a perfect word to use. When dealing with time there are only actions taken. All actions have positive and negative consequences in the grand scheme of things."

"Not that that makes it okay that there are countless suffering Gretchens out there," Gretchen in the purple robe said coldly.

"We get over it," the more experienced Gretchen said.

"What I am most concerned about," Woah Te continued, "is that you lacked the compassion to stop yourself in the first place. You've lived countless lives, all of us travelers have, remembering each of those lives should give you a sense of the importance of life. And a perspective unwilling to wipe it out so coldly for your own gain."

"I don't remember most of my past lives. They fade, like memories when you get old."

We came to a door, once again carved with intricate detail, it depicted a snake wrapped around the base of a tree. The snake's mouth was open and its fangs spread out to be the leafy branches of a tree. It was a strange visual illusion and I couldn't spot the trick before Woah Te opened the door with a creak.

Woah Te walked through the door hunching his large brown wings down to fit. Everyone else walked through fine.

The room had soft grass covering the floor like carpet. Foliage grew up around the edges blooming with red and orange bell-shaped flowers. A strange plant with large elephant ear leaves sprouted in the center of the room before our eyes.

It was a square table, or at least a close enough approximation, with a chair-shaped leaf on each side.

Woah Te took a seat on the one with the thinnest backrest letting his wings stretch out. He rolled his shoulders back as if he was making himself comfortable. Both Gretchens took a seat on either side of the owl facing each other. Which left me the last seat with my back to the door having to face the strange owl creature.

I draped my trench coat over the back of the chair. When the leaf didn't collapse from its weight I slowly sat down, still hesitant that the leaves would hold my weight. They did. It was far more comfortable than the previous seat I'd found inside the Celestial Mother Tree.

"Memories don't fade, Todd," Gretchen, the one in black, said. "I've lived a few dozen lives already and I can pluck every memory, every moment, out of them like it was yesterday. My timeline is like a movie in my mind. I can pick any timestamp, go there, and experience it like it's happening now."

"My memories from childhood are coming back as well," the other Gretchen verified. "Things I'd lost I can remember, even see, exactly where I left them."

"That's not how it works for me," I said. "And I don't know if I want it to be." Every mistake I ever made would come back in full clarity. Including every gruesome death, I'd dealt to Gretchen.

"That is what concerns us," Woah Te said. "It's why we wanted you back here. We'd like to look into your mind and see if we can recover your memories. Without them you'll become lost in time, unable to remember where you've been, what you've done. You'll have endless power without any sympathy to hold your actions back."

"Your memories fight the existential dread of the expansive universe," Gretchen, in the purple robe, said. "It's why I felt better after traveling. Also, maybe if Woah Te can recover your memories we'll know why you killed me so many times."

"I did it to have someone special to me in the universe. I did it to overlap my own consciousness, that's what my death unlocked."

"You could've gotten the same effect without dragging us into it," Gretchen in black said.

"And if you had your memories you would be able to feel the beauty of life," Woah Te added.

"Life isn't beautiful," I groaned. "It's pointless suffering against inevitable nothingness."

"Without the right perspective that's true. But if you could remember all your many past lives, each moment big and small, across millennia you'd see how rare and hopeful and meaningful even the smallest actions can be."

"That's the kind of crap people want you to take on faith," I said.

"You can feel the expansive nothingness of infinite time and the endless multiverse, correct?" Woah Te asked patiently.

I nodded.

"You no longer have to take that on faith. Once your memories return to you you'll feel the meaning of the world as unquestioningly as the existentialism. There is no faith needed."

I didn't like it. Being bitter about the pointlessness of it all was uncomfortable but easy. Having knowledge, tangible memories, about the quality of life seemed like a responsibility I didn't want to take on.

"And if I don't do this?" I asked.

"Then Mrs. Smith won't return your ability to travel," Woah Te said.

Gretchen held up her right arm, the purple worm still wrapped around and embedded into it. "The glowing orb floating inside. It's your ability to travel. Stole it from you in the school cafeteria."

"You were the void figure haunting me?" I asked.

"I was following myself," Gretchen gestured to the college-aged version of herself across the table. "You just happened to be around. We drag ourselves back here. But mask ourselves as void figures to keep from impacting the universes we enter. Especially in delicate situations like awakening our travel abilities."

"And you just took away my ability to travel?"

"Seemed the safest thing to do. Keep you from disappearing into the multiverse again." Gretchen said. "Plus I was sitting across the table from me when I admitted it in my own past."

"Yeah," I said curious turning to the Gretchen in purple. "If you two are sharing this timeline does that mean that you died?"

"The Celestial Mother Tree sits outside of time," Woah Te responded. "Actions like dying and overlapping your timeline are dangerous and ill-advised."

"We covered it in orientation," Gretchen in purple said with a small grin. "Which you conveniently forgot."

I rolled my eyes at Gretchen.

"And since I already saw how this conversation is going to go I know I am not needed," the Gretchen in black said getting up from her leaf chair.

"We agreed that you'd return Toodd's ability once his memories are returned," Woah Te said. His wings arched on his back and his airy voice sounded almost flustered.

"I know. I'm not leaving the tree. You can find me when I'm needed." Gretchen stood near the flowering foliage around the edge of the room. Eventually, a door appeared and she walked out.

I was sick of not knowing as much as everyone else in this room. I was sick of others knowing how my life was going to go. I'd finally figured out the answer to whether or not there were other travelers like me.

There were. And they were all as rigid as their uncomfortable wooden chairs.

I was a reasonable person. Anything I did had a reason behind it. Returning my memories would only expose those reasons. I could bring comfort to Gretchen and give her a better reason for why she died in so many universes. Maybe my memories would bring comfort to me as well.

At the very least I could prove the leather jacket-wearing version of Gretchen wrong and make her come back. A minor inconvenience but all I could muster in this situation.

"I'll do it."

Woah Te hooted in agreement. Vines began to grow from the leafy canopy of the ceiling towards me. My leaf chair began to recline as if it were reacting to a moving light source.

"These vines will connect you to the Celestial Mother Tree," Woah Te explained, "and she will do what she can to unlock your memories."

I nodded in agreement. Barely phased by the statement. It was hardly the wildest statement the owl man had made today.

11

I ran to the bridge of the ship still in my bloody surgery gown, I urgently needed to get to the captain.

I piloted the ship, sitting next to the captain, keeping an eye on the telemetry as we hovered at the edge of the local planet's orbit, ready to escape into space at the captain's order.

I captained the ship, waiting for the medical examiner to send me the results from the xenobiologist's surgery.

I used to be a xenobiologist. Now I lay dead on the operating room table.

Three floors below I was a chef cooking dinner for the crew, fettuccini al burro, my wife's favorite. Unaware of all the chaos going on around me.

I was the chef's wife still in our small cabin laying in bed with another man, the security officer who just returned from the local planet safely.

Was it cheating if I was also the security officer? Grateful to return safely from yet another dangerous exploration of the universe's many exoplanets. Not every one that left made it back alive.

I will be upset at myself. I, the chef, would never forgive either of us for cheating. Until he woke up from his amnesia and realized we were all the same person. We were all Todd Rungson.

There were three hundred twenty-seven people on the exploration ship. Each one of them was a version of me who'd forgotten their past. We each coincidentally enrolled for a position on this ship. Guided by a force I could only notice once I remembered the lives I'd lived.

And even then I couldn't put my finger on them.

I lived three hundred twenty-seven lives at once, some long, some cut short. Each life was a blink of an eye, but the memories stuck with me as I experienced them. And when the final crew member died, a custodian officer who enrolled young and lived a long life eventually retiring to hike the alien mountains of Sarin V, I woke up.

Vines that connected me to the Celestial Mother Tree hovered above my face as they receded from my scalp. Woah Te and his looming brown wings stood over me. Gretchen held my hand, for comfort or encouragement I didn't remember.

Which was a shame because the whole point of these exercises was to remember.

I was still in the forested room of the tree. Still reclined in the leaf chair. The table had wilted, a new chair had sprung up so Gretchen could sit closer to me. The red and yellow flowers around the perimeter were in full bloom.

"I felt it again this time," I said. Gretchen let go of my hand as I spoke. "I felt something guiding my live's actions." It was like an invisible magnetic force pushing me towards enlisting on that starship. It'd shown up every time the Celestial Mother Tree connected to me for the memory procedure.

"Do you remember all of your lives?" Woah Te asked. It was the only thing he was interested in. He wanted all my memories flooding back. As if I could even handle that. I could barely handle remembering an entire ship of lifetimes.

"No," I groaned. This was something like the eighth or ninth attempt. Even that number I couldn't remember exactly. "Give me a few more tries. I am starting to feel the compassion of multiple lifetimes you spoke of."

The crew's memories stuck in my mind like the scenes of a movie. But that wasn't enough for Woah Te.

I thought it was wonderful. The memories were doing their job. It was hard to be bitter about my insignificance in the multiverse when I could feel my interconnected lives stretch out for centuries.

Sure some people died young or failed to make a dent in the universe, but they were loved and impactful to the crew members they served with. And like a bolt of lightning before it connects to the ground their actions tendrilled out into the void. And maybe that moment before lightning strikes the ground is where the wonder of the universe exists.

"The woodpeckers say don't beat your head against a piece of bark if there are no bugs underneath," Woah Te replied.

The vines began to climb back up into the leafy canopy.

Each time we performed the procedure memories came back. The bandwidth of lives I could live nearly doubled every time. At first, it was a couple lives, then ten, then fifty, then a hundred. Now it was a ship of people. If I kept connecting to the tree it'd be a planet's worth of people. How far away could a universe of people and then a multiverse of lives be after that?

"I want to do it again," I told the owl.

"We are done." Despite Woah Te's words sounding hollow, the statement was firm.

It didn't stop me from arguing with him. "I'm taking on more lives each time, I'll get all my memories back eventually if we keep this up. Are you worried about running out of time?" I gave the owl a wry smile.

His beak did not bend to reciprocate, nor did his mood. "This is not an exercise in remembering some lives. Something is blocking your ability to remember all of your lives. Each time the Mother Tree tries to remove the block she fails. This procedure can not repair you."

"Is there another procedure we can try?" Gretchen asked.

"We have no other procedures," Woah Te replied. "This is not a problem we run into often."

"Then have Gretchen give me my powers back and let me go find a solution somewhere else in the multiverse."

"We cannot afford to lose you again. I will be telling Gretchen not to return your ability to travel."

Based on our last interaction I doubted my pleas would overrule Woah Te's stance.

"I won't get lost. I won't forget the goal of remembering my lives now that I know it's possible. And now that I know its value." It was nice being able to feel the interconnectedness of life through the years. "I won't forget this place either. How could I?"

"You've forgotten it once before." Woah Te's words were slow and airy and their truth haunted me. "Rest for now. The Mother Tree will show you to your rooms."

The sound of rustling leaves and cracking wood drew my attention across the forest clearing we were in.

A wooden door appeared, a roaring bear on its back legs with its front paws raised high was carved into the door. Was the artwork the Mother Tree trying to show her frustration at how unreceptive I was to her procedure?

If so I agreed with her frustration.

"I will find you after I rest," Woah Te said. "Maybe we will have a new approach by then." The owl stretched his wings. He flapped his wings with enough force that my jacket blew off the back of my chair Woah Te flew through a small gap in the canopy leaves that I could have sworn wasn't there previously.

But who knows? My memory, apparently, wasn't as good as it should be.

I picked up my jacket with a frustrated groan.

"How are you doing?" Gretchen asked.

"Peachy considering I can't travel, I can't remember anything, and I've exhausted all the resources available to a tree outside of time and space. You?"

"I'm still interested in knowing why you needed to kill me. But I'm feeling better about my place in the universe as my younger memories come back."

I pushed the roaring bear door open, it smelled like freshly cut wood, and Gretchen followed me through. Behind the door was an endless hallway with wood paneling just like the last one we walked through, despite the door being in a different place in the room.

"I'm sorry I killed you," I said as we walked down the long hall.

Gretchen didn't immediately respond.

"I hope my memory comes back and I can give you a satisfying reason for why you died," I continued. "But I also know there isn't anything I can say that will make what I did okay. I'm sorry that I put all those versions of you through so much pain, along with your parents and friends and god knows what misery they dished out to others in their grief."

I didn't know the details of each of those lives but I could vividly imagine the actions they took now that I remembered my past lives in such vivid detail.

"I'm sorry I ruined your life, in those universes, and the lives of those who loved you. I hid behind the guise of their lives only lasting a few decades in the face of infinity. To me, then, it looked like nothing."

My nose wrinkled and my lips tried to force themselves into a frown. I fought them back wanting to keep a straight face for Gretchen.

"But to them, it was all they had... and I ruined it."

Wood split and I thought I saw sawdust flutter through the air for a moment. I looked away, uninterested in what was carved into the door right now. I looked at Gretchen instead.

"I'm sorry I caused so much chaos. It is unforgivable."

Gretchen looked up at me and smiled softly. "You're right. What you did was awful."

She shook the sleeve of her purple robe so her finger could hook onto the wide cuff. She lifted the cloth up to my cheek and wiped away a tear I hadn't cared to notice.

"But according to the other version of me I'll forgive you, eventually. And I'm starting to see how that might fall into place."

"How?" I asked.

"Don't worry about it," she reached out for the door to push it open. Her hand landed on the antler of a stag.

I looked at the Mother Tree's carving. A bear rested its head, eyes closed on the back of a large deer whose branching antlers reached out of the door.

The deer's gaze was aimed up. The carved pupils of its eyes seemingly made eye contact with me. To me, he seemed proud, like a parent who'd put an energetic toddler to bed.

12

The room we entered was a rocky cave with moss covering a few of the surfaces and glowing mushrooms hanging from the ceiling like small chandeliers. My recent life as a scientist on an exploration ship told me that this cave had not formed naturally. Not entirely surprising since it seemed to me that the Mother Tree was generating doors, halls, and rooms on command.

The rocks were slate gray with sharp angles. Some jutted out of the ground, unlike any stalagmite that would form over time, which made sense as this tree was allegedly outside of time.

To our right was a rock that was counter height with a taller bar height surface behind it. To the left, there was a four-legged table intricately carved out of wood.

Despite being a cave it was well lit. The glowing mushrooms hung from the ceiling in every part of the cave. They threw off a soft yellow light. There was a musty smell in the air, perhaps from the mushrooms or the moss. Water dripped at a steady rate from somewhere in the room. There was something about the unnatural cave that I recognized but couldn't put my finger on.

"It's my apartment!" Gretchen sounded excited to find a place so familiar in this strange world.

She walked further into the apartment brushing her hand over a moss-covered rock that was a very close replica of her couch, the one I'd sat next to for hours trying to teach her to travel.

She plopped down on the sofa and kicked her feet up onto a coffee table-shaped rock. "Wow! I think this moss one is more comfortable than the original original."

She was right, it was a replica of the college apartments we'd recently lived in.

One bedroom door was behind the bar and it entered into the living room. It was the familiar intricately carved wood door. A mother bear with three small cubs following her was carved into it.

I checked the dining room and found the other bedroom door. This one had the stag with massive antlers grazing lazily on some grass. Grass so finely carved that the slightest touch could break it off the door.

I went to push it open since that was the room I'd come out of to find Gretchen cooking chicken soup hours and lifetimes ago.

"Hey, that's my room. You take Marissa's," Gretchen said. She jumped up from the couch and marched up to me her loose-fitting purple robe flowed with each step.

"In my apartment, my room opened into the dining room as well," I said. It was likely the reason the roommate let me monopolize the table with a mess of costume supplies.

"My Todd had a room that opened to the dining room. You get the bear. It fits you better anyway."

I pushed at the door but it didn't budge.

Gretchen looked at me a satisfied smile on her lips.

I began to ask, "How does a bear fit—"

The splintering of wood cut me off.

I looked at the front door. It stood in the same place. The back of the door was simple carved paneling as if to imply we could leave but it wouldn't be as interesting of a direction to go. The sound of creaking wood came from the living room. Another plain door opened where the glass door of the balcony should have been.

Gretchen walked in wearing her leather jacket, cross expression, and the purple glowing worm wrapped around her wrist. She lazily looked around the room taking it in. She wasn't judging the space but seemed to be sizing up an old friend.

She sat back on the couch with a sigh and kicked her feet up on the coffee table rock. "The bear is supposed to be yours Todd," she finally said.

"Are you staying here too?" I asked.

The Gretchen standing next to me pushed on the stag door and it creaked open at her touch. She cracked it just enough to slip inside and I could barely get a peek into it before it shut in my face.

"No. And neither are you. Take a seat," she gestured across the table to the bare stone floor of the room.

The ground cracked and the shape of an armchair rose up out of the rock. Moss spread out from the cracks that usually held coins and remotes.

I sat on the new armchair. Gretchen was right, the moss was far more comfortable than the original. It was the most comfortable seat I'd taken inside this tree.

"Can we ask the Celestial Mother Tree to make anything for us?" I asked.

Gretchen shrugged as if I'd asked how she was enjoying the weather.

"Where am I sleeping if I'm not staying here?" I asked.

"Wherever you want. I'm giving you your powers back."

That was simpler than I expected. It took no cajoling, bribing, or pleading on my part. Which immediately made me suspicious of a condition or a trap. "Why?" I asked. "I'm not fixed, according to Woah Te."

"But you feel better, yeah? Less murderous?" Gretchen asked with a rare grin.

"Yeah, I'm sorry I murdered you so much. I shouldn't have put all those—"

She waved her hand to dismiss my apology. "I've heard it before, in the hallway, it's okay I got over it."

"Why return my ability to travel though?"

"Woah Te, that younger version of me, everyone else around her thinks having memories back is some grand blessing. I'm starting to think it's a blessing with a cost. If you want this it's yours," she gestured at the glowing worm around her wrist. "Get out of here if you want."

"What even is that thing?" Multiverse orientation hadn't come back and this version of Gretchen might be interested in sharing.

"It's a nitthog, a worm that lives at the roots of the Celestial Mother Tree."

"And this neat hog can hold my ability to travel?" I looked at the glowing orb that swam around inside the worm. "In its stomach? I really wish I could retake that orientation."

"No. You don't. Trust me." Gretchen looked more stern and foreboding than normal.

"I'll give you the long and short," she added before I could protest. "Most living things have a physical body and a conscious body. Usually, they're linked really tight, and when one dies so does the other. Matter breaks down into smaller atoms and redistributes into the universe. Same thing happens with your consciousness.

"Your conscious body has different parts like memories, emotions, and," she gestured at her wrist, "your cosmic sense of direction."

"So your pet worm basically bit off my ethereal arm," I said concerned about how permanent that amputation might be in the long run.

"He grew up outside of time at the roots of the mother tree and feeds on conscious matter. The avians bred a few to do specific tasks. One of those tasks was to remove the ability to travel from others."

"And they have that authority because...?"

"They're a wise and ancient people."

I looked at Gretchen skeptically.

"... and they got to the tree first."

"So you're going to go against these wise and ancient people. Why?"

"The more I learn about the multiverse and our place in it as travelers..." Gretchen pulled her feet down from the coffee table and leaned forward on the couch, "the more I think it's no great loss to lose your memory."

She reached her arm out to me. The purple nitthog, infused in her arm like an overgrown tumor, was within my reach. Gretchen looked at me, brow furrowed and focused.

I didn't like the look in her hazel eyes. They seemed to look through me. As if I was nothing but a pawn in her scheme. I didn't like it.

But I didn't like being without my powers either. Trapped here, insignificant to Woah Te who refused to explain anything or truly help me. The owl gave up after only a few attempts.

"Just grab it," Gretchen said.

If I had my powers back, I wouldn't have to leave. I could stick around. Learn more. Try whatever new experimental help Woah Te might come up with.

I reached my arm out to grab Gretchen's wrist. The orb stopped aimlessly swimming around in the nitthog's gut. Inside the stomach, it moved towards me like my hand was a powerful magnet.

"What the hell are you doing?" Gretchen interrupted from the dining room. She was no longer in purple robes or pajamas. She wore new blue jeans and sneakers. But she still had the same old t-shirt with the matrix of superhero faces on it.

I grabbed the nitthog. Terrified the opportunity would pass. The glowing orb disappeared from the worm. I expected to feel the ability return, like my lungs were inflated with breath of fresh air. But my cosmic sense of direction was hardly perceptible.

I took a deep breath and reached out for a universe to travel to. I wanted to go home, to my Fortress of Solitude. Where I'd be free of strange trees and owl people.

"Oh no. You're not going anywhere!" Gretchen rushed from the dining room to my side.

I kept breathing reaching out to feel my escape to my fortress.

The Gretchen who'd just returned my powers sat back on the couch and kicked her feet up again like she was sinking in to read a good book. The nitthog shriveled and morphed into her skin leaving a purple tattoo around her wrist. She smiled at me knowingly. After all, she'd already lived this moment. Just from a different perspective.

I hooked onto the world I wanted to travel to. I felt the armchair of the space station under me. Relieved that I could disappear at any moment I let the thought go.

"I'm not going anywhere," I said.

"Why'd you return his powers?" Gretchen asked herself, a doubtful scowl starting to form on her brow.

"We trust him now," she responded. "Remember? He apologized." She took a deep breath and relaxed into the couch. "And you should probably go soon. The avians won't be thrilled about my decision to return your abilities."

"Then why'd you do it?!" Gretchen repeated.

"Because we need him. I need him. And trust him. But—"

Wood splintered and cut her off. Every door in the room disappeared replaced with blank slate gray walls.

Gretchen looked at me. "But you shouldn't trust her. Not yet." She took a deep breath and disappeared.

"You're not going anywhere," the remaining Gretchen said. She stood over me as I sat in the moss-covered armchair and placed her hand on my shoulder as if to hold me in place.

"You can't keep me here. There are answers out—"

Wood splintered again. This time a blank door appeared where the balcony window should've been.

"I need to find answers, my memories. Woah Te won't let me."

"Then I'm coming with you." She clutched my shoulder tighter as if she was hanging onto me.

I took a deep breath and focused on my fortress. It was a place to start looking for answers, or at least regroup. I'd never taken anyone there. There was never anyone to take.

And it was my private space, like my mind, I didn't want people inside it rummaging around and breaking things. Not that it meant everything stayed in one piece in the end.

The door creaked open. Woah Te filed in along with two other avians that were hawk-like with their sharp beaks and sleek feathered heads.

I took a final breath. I focused on my destination. I was going to take Gretchen home. For better or worse.

13

I sat reclined on a padded leather sectional couch. It was likely real leather, at this time in Earth's history, the material was common, affordable, and stylish. I held a book of crosswords in my hand, the current puzzle was half filled out with little pencil marks.

Music played from a speaker somewhere, it was a long drawn out, tune about love or the lack of it. It was one of Gretchen's favorites.

Early morning sun came in through the living room's large eastward-facing windows. It got hot in the summer but these early spring days the extra light and heat were appreciated.

I wore an old paint-stained sweatshirt with a few holes in it. My sweatpants were in better condition and my fuzzy house shoes were practically brand new. If I remembered correctly they were a Christmas present from our son to replace the old tattered pair I'd worn for the past eight years.

The living room was decorated with an assortment of family pictures and souvenirs from our global travels. Gretchen had fought me for years to "tidy" the place up and pick a cohesive theme for the main living room. But to me, the theme was already cohesive, a life with the woman I love and the family we created.

The living room opened up into the kitchen. Brown granite countertops covered every surface including the bar and the island. The fridge hummed away in the corner of the room, its old compressor rattled against the frame. I'd replace it in the summer, but right now the incessant sound was a comforting reminder to make the most of what I had before it broke down completely.

The entire room smelled like coffee. Gretchen just finished making us a fresh cup and was decanting it out of our glass pour-over carafe. It was a sleekly designed flower-vase-shaped brewer that we'd had since college. Unfortunately, it eventually shattered a shame and a loss. And despite its importance, for some reason, I couldn't remember how we broke it.

I looked to Gretchen and gave her a pleasant smile. She wore a fuzzy bathrobe over a t-shirt. Her hair, with streaks of silver in it, was pulled up in a bun.

We were both older. We had plenty of grey hairs but only a few wrinkles so far. We would soon be grandparents if my memory served. We were happily retired thanks to a few well-placed investments guided by a quick trip I took to this multiverse's future in college.

Gretchen looked back at me but did not return my smile. Her eyes were wide and horrified in shock. She dropped the carafe, still half filled with fresh coffee. It bounced off the hard counter and onto the tile floor. A shatter echoed through the house.

"It's okay," I said getting up from the recliner. The metal squeaked as the footrest went down and my knees popped as I stood up to walk to the kitchen.

"Where are we?" Gretchen asked. Her brow began to furrow a rare expression in this universe.

"This is the universe where we lived our lives together. After I gave up my life to save you from the SUV." I opened the pantry door where we kept a broom and mop.

"After you killed me countless times and eventually yourself." She rephrased the information like it was merely a news report. "Why'd you want to go here?"

"As far as I can tell this is what those deaths were for. So that, if only for a lifetime, I would know what it was like to have someone who meant the world to me in this expansive multiverse."

Gretchen gracefully stepped over the shattered glass at her feet as I began to mop up the puddle of coffee. She was luckily also wearing house shoes on this crisp spring morning.

"We have kids, three of them," I gestured to the pictures in the living room. They ranged from school portraits to candid shots of vacations we'd gone on. "We're about to have grandkids over the next few years." Glass rattled under my mop as it slid on the tile.

"I can't imagine," Gretchen said picking up a picture from a ski trip. We sat on a ski lift, frosted pine trees around us. You could barely see more than our smiles under the bundles of clothes and tinted goggles, but they were as bright as the white snow around us. "Todd followed me to college, I figured we'd peter out. Go our own way. I don't know."

"We did a few times, in a couple universes," I put the coffee-stained mop and glass shards in a bucket. The eminent threat was over. The version of me that lived here could take care of the rest. "After this universe, I never could seem to get the hang of keeping us together."

I walked over to Gretchen who was looking at a family picture. The five of us standing in front of a waterfall covered up in rain gear. Not that the gear kept us from getting soaked that day.

"What are their names?" She asked. "What are they like?"

"Charlie is the oldest, she's a museum curator in the Midwest. She wants to be a painter but it's hard to do both. I keep telling her to quit and paint but she wants to be independent and doesn't want to use our money to do it."

"That's thoughtful of her," Gretchen said.

I shrugged. "Being able to visit the future makes investing easy. I'm not sure why anyone wouldn't take advantage of being born into a family that lucky."

"Maybe she doesn't want to owe you."

"What's there to owe? We dragged her into existence. Least I can do is make her comfortable."

Gretchen laughed in shock. "What about the other two?"

"Erik is the middle child. He does investment banking, not sure where we went wrong with him. His wife Angela is pregnant with twins. He's pretty clever. Eventually, he catches on that the well-placed investments I made in college, along with the rest of our portfolio, were improbably lucky."

"You tell him about your abilities?"

"Nah. I told him I was psychic. It sounded just as ridiculous. He didn't press it, didn't want to get in trouble with the SEC. I think he assumes it was some kind of insider trading. He always liked rational explanations."

"So none of your kids know you can travel through the multiverse?" Gretchen sounded shocked.

"Nah," I dismissed, "I told you, but who knows if you actually believed me."

"You told the Gretchen that belongs to this universe," she clarified.

"Sure, yeah. But it didn't seem prudent to make it a family affair. Our youngest is Hannah she's about to graduate with a degree in industrial engineering. Not that she ever uses it."

"What does she do then?"

"She will mostly spend her time traveling. She tries different hobbies: writing, photography, singing, plays a dozen different instruments, and speaks at least a half dozen languages."

"Hmm," Gretchen said almost dismissively.

"You think she's spoiled."

"I don't think anything. They're all strangers to me."

"The Gretchen of this universe thought that," I clarified. "But like I said, why not take advantage of your luck? I always thought she would've enjoyed traveling the multiverse. She could spend lifetimes perfecting each of her hobbies."

"And you never told her?"

"And dangle a carrot she'd never reach in front of her?" I sighed. "If I was going to tell anyone it would've been her. But she passed away in a mountaineering accident. She was only 47."

"That's awful. I'm sorry." Gretchen said.

"It was. I abused my powers trying to convince her not to go." I shook my head. "Not a story for today. It's a few years away from where we are right now." I took a deep breath to hold back some unwelcome tears.

"You had a good life here," Gretchen finally said putting down the last of the framed pictures I had on display. "Not sure it's the life I'd want to live though."

"This Gretchen was different from you. Significantly different."

"More gullible and easily manipulated?" Gretchen scoffed she walked towards the kitchen and reached over the bar for the last cup of coffee.

"More accepting, patient. Trusting," I added with a smile.

The coffee was in my cup. It had an MC Escher painting that I loved printed on it. Gretchen was always creeped out by the optical illusion and refused to use it even if it was the last clean mug. To me, it reminded me of the twists and turns of the multiverse.

It didn't bother the Gretchen in front of me. She sipped the coffee and sat back on a bar stool.

"We're at an impasse you know?" She said after a few sips.

"How so?" I took my reclined seat back on the couch.

"Part of orientation is that they put a tracking memory in you. Woah Te could easily follow me here using that memory."

I looked at Gretchen confused.

"There's your material body and your conscious body. Your conscious body is what travel—"

"I got that spiel from the other version of you. How do they track you with a memory?"

"Your memories are part of your conscious body. They had me look into a bright orb at the center of the mother tree. Woah Te explained that with that orb in my memory, they can find me anywhere in the multiverse. In case I get lost in time."

"Like I did."

"Except you don't remember orientation. So, they can't track you."

"Lucky me," I said dryly.

"Except Woah Te hasn't shown up yet and in all your memories of your life in this universe I assume you didn't see any avians."

"No. I would've remembered that."

"Maybe it's because I traveled with you. But if I return to Woah Te he'll show up here and capture you. Take you back to the mother tree where you won't cause any more harm."

"Which would be your preferred solution?" I asked.

"Historically you've been a danger to me, or at least Gretchens like me."

"Erik would say: past performance is no guarantee of future results," I said with a smile.

Gretchen was unamused. Busy contemplating her conundrum. She took a few more sips of coffee then put my mug down. "I'm going to leave you. Maybe try to go back to the mother tree at a time before I return your powers for some reason. I'll live a life with my Todd, hopefully, it will be as meaningful as this life you have here with Gretchen."

"I hope it is," I said with sincerity.

"You've got to promise me two things though, if I'm not going to turn you in."

"Sure," I said with an agreeable shrug.

"I'm serious. Or so help me God—or whoever is running this chaos—I will hunt you through the multiverse again."

Gretchen eyebrows were wrinkled, stern, and serious. Her eyes had the ferocity of a Valkyrie.

"One," she put up her index finger, "don't kill or harm another Gretchen." She held up her middle finger, "Two, figure out what's going on with your memory so that you don't get lost again."

I wanted to agree immediately, but immediacy might weaken the agreement. Even if she wasn't the Gretchen I knew and loved I cared about her like a close friend. Hell, she might be the only other human who can travel the multiverse like me. That was a bond of some sort.

After a moment of solemn thought, I agreed. "I won't hurt anymore Gretchens. And I'll figure out the memories, even if I don't ever find you an answer."

"I'm over getting answers. It's in the past. Whatever the past means to people like us." Gretchen said as she took a deep breath.

"Good luck on your travels," I said.

"You too," Gretchen replied between breaths. "You're the one who's going to need it."

Gretchen exhaled and her face went from serious to confused in an instant. The default—no, the Gretchen that belonged to this universe had returned.

I closed my eyes and took a deep breath to avoid having to answer any questions. I imagined my satellite fortress, the silent place I could go to start the hunt for my memories.

"Wait. Don't go yet," Gretchen said.

14

I opened my eyes, shocked to hear the Gretchen that belonged to this universe interrupt my traveling. She rushed around the brown sectional couch towards me. The long tail of her bathrobe flowed behind her in her haste. She sat next to me on the couch and clutched my wrist.

Physically nothing about this Gretchen had changed. Her silver hair was still pulled up in a bun. She still wore the comfortable morning clothes of a slow day of retirement. But her posture was different.

She was not confused. She was intent.

"I'm going with you," she said. Her right hand gripped firmly on my wrist.

"I'm not going anywhere," I replied nonchalantly. I laid my head back on the reclined seat of the couch. "I'm just resting."

"Bull," Gretchen said flatly squeezing me almost uncomfortably.

I looked down at her grip and saw a purple tattoo around her wrist. I looked up at Gretchen shocked.

"You going to take my powers away again?" I asked. "How long has it been since you left me here?"

This must be a version of the Gretchen that could travel, the Gretchen I lived with never had a tattoo like that. But I couldn't tell how far into her life she was. Maybe I broke the promise and she was here to exact her revenge before it could happen. If that already happened this wouldn't stop me but that didn't mean Gretchen wouldn't try.

"I just returned your powers to you. When I left the moss couch I came here."

"Because you knew that this is where I would take the younger version of you."

"Exactly."

"So why are you back?" I asked. My focused breath and the images of my Fortress of Solitude faded.

"Because I'm running from Woah Te too. I doubt he's thrilled about me letting you loose in the multiverse again. And you said avians never appeared in this universe."

"But the tracking memory. You lead them right to me."

"So let's go," Gretchen shook my arm urgently. "If you lead the travel they won't be able to follow us."

"You told me not to trust—"

The room began to shake. Static fuzzed around the edges of my vision. Soon void figures, the avians masking themselves to avoid impacting this timeline, would loom over me.

Like a child trying to hide from danger, I squeezed my eyes shut. Gretchen tightened her grip on my arm. I took a deep breath, before the void figures paralyzed me in time, and aimed for my satellite home.

I hooked onto the sensation of sitting in my high-backed chair in front of the towering monitors of the satellite's computers. I took deep breaths quickly but not rushed.

After a short moment, Gretchen's grip disappeared from my arm. I'd lost her in time or space I didn't know. I opened my eyes to look for her.

She stood next to me, in the chrome-covered satellite I called home. Gretchen wore her short black leather jacket, a blue shirt, and tennis shoes that squeaked with every step she took across the smooth metal floors.

She walked to the window where Jupiter loomed. I spun my chair to watch her take in the sight.

Small hockey puck-shaped cleaning bots hummed as they scrubbed the floor and walls. Notifications chimed quietly on the monitors reminding me that a spacecraft had docked hours ago and I needed to unload it.

I hated to leave the station unattended. With time under my control, I would have preferred to appear here as soon as I unintentionally left to visit Gretchen in the bathtub. However, the rushed nature of the travel caused me to lose precision. Unfortunately, void figures seemed to do that to me.

I got up from my seat, ignoring the monitor's notification, and slung my heavy trench coat over the back of the chair tired of having its weight on my back if only for a moment.

My heavy-soled boots clomped across the metal floor as I walked to the center of the circular room to the recessed floor where the couches sat. Cloth covered in sky blue, a rare color off planet.

I laid down on the couch, the memory foam padding conforming to my body, and closed my eyes. I was exhausted, not physically but mentally. My mind raced, there was no shortage of problems to solve. And despite being able to travel through time I didn't feel like there was enough time for me. Especially with the avians on our tails.

"It's beautiful," Gretchen said gesturing at the gas giant above us.

I grunted an acknowledgement eyes still closed.

"We went to space once," Gretchen said. "Todd and I." Gretchen's voice echoed through the cavernous satellite.

There'd never been anyone to speak to here before. My voice commands to the computer were the only quiet words ever spoken here. And I never paid attention to the resonance of my own voice.

"It wasn't anything fancy like this," Gretchen continued. Her sneakers squeaked as she walked down the steps into the seating pit. "It was just a quick flight far enough outside of Earth's atmosphere which was technically considered space. Todd loved it though."

I opened my eyes and turned my head to the side to look at her. Her brow wasn't furrowed or angry, she seemed almost relaxed sitting on the couch across from me.

I sat up. Frustrated.

"You told me not to trust you yet here I am with you in my Fortress of Solitude." I wasn't exactly shouting but my irritation was unobscured. "You let me escape the tree but then you show up immediately after with the multiverse police in tow. What's your game?"

"Fortress of Solitude. That's cute." Gretchen said with a tiny chuckle. "Guess the solitude is out the window now though. Do you have a spare room?"

"Oh no. You're not staying. I'm getting answers from you and then you're leaving."

"You don't want me to leave." Gretchen unlaced her tennis shoes as she spoke, eventually peeling off her thin neon green and pink athletic socks.

I didn't like she was starting to make herself comfortable.

"While I've got this tracking memory in me any travel I do will stand out like a Quester at a Galaxy Gang convention to the avians."

I looked across the seating pit at her. The moment was all but silent between us except for the computer's continuous notification ping.

"Todd would've loved that," she added. "Either way, they'll know exactly where this place is. Putting the fortress part of your name to the test."

I groaned. As much at her as at myself. Of all the places in the multiverse I could've fled to this was where I returned. I could've left her on an icy alien mountain on Sarin V or in a random tower in Galleria Valley. But I brought her here.

"It's not like you haven't been here before," I said remembering the void figure that visited me.

"I haven't. It's nice though. Todd would've loved it." She shrugged her jacket off and it slipped from the couch onto the floor.

"I do love it." I stood up in an attempt to make a point and began pacing around the seating area. "And I love that it's not infested with controlling birds. And now you're just going to disappear and lead them here." The carpeted floor padded my steps and I felt like my point was limited, just like any control I had over this situation.

"I'm not going anywhere." Gretchen sat back cross-legged and comfortable on the couch.

I doubtfully grunted at her. That was like a cat promising they wouldn't bother you in the bathroom. Lasted as long as their next whim.

"I told you in the cave apartment that I thought you were on the right track with losing your memories."

"You just made me promise to figure out what is going on with my memory," I reminded her.

A cleaning bot hummed between my feet the sanitizer it used wafted to my nose and I wished it could clean my hands of this situation.

"And I stand by that. Because I'm hoping that when you figure out what's going on you'll help me wipe this tracking memory from my mind. Until then I'm not going anywhere you don't take me."

The computer continued to beep, reminding me of the docked shipment, and increasing my irritation.

"And if I just grab you and transport you to some random planet in space and time?" I asked as I walked out of the conversation pit which was easier to exit than this conversation.

"That'd probably be easier for me," Gretchen shouted from behind me. "Just pick me up when you've figured it all out. I would only have to wait a moment if you return seconds after you dropped me off."

"Assuming I remember where I left you," I muttered as I walked down the 4 o'clock hallway toward the docking bay. My boots echoed down the space station's tube-like hallway.

Apparently so did my voice because a pitter patter of bare feed came from behind. Their cadence sounded like Gretchen was jogging behind me to catch up.

I didn't look behind me to confirm. I took longer strides to get to the edge of the station quicker.

"Nice place," Gretchen said once she was next to me. "You going to give me a tour?" She barely sounded out of breath.

We'd reached the edge of the hallway to the ring of docks where shipments I sent to myself arrived. I could see a small red spaceship the size of a small barn linked to the ring of the satellite.

"What's on that?" Gretchen asked pointing at the ship.

"Dunno," I said. "But I'm hoping it's a shipment of whiskey. Or something to make this headache of a roommate situation more bearable."

15

The cavernous dock echoed with the sound of splintering wood as I used a crowbar to open the new shipment.

My cold breath left a cloud of fog in front of my face. I wished I had my jacket. But I'd already spent a trip across the satellite to get mag boots and a crowbar to open this thing. I wasn't wasting another trip just to stave off a little hypothermia.

I had to get the mag boots in order to walk across the deck of the ship. The boots were able to attach to the steel floor giving me leverage while I opened the massive crate in front of me. The artificial gravity field of the satellite didn't extend past its outer ring. Leaving docking ships to either provide their own or be zero-g like old-timey spaceships.

This delivery ship went with the latter option. No artificial gravity field and barely enough insulation to keep the cold of space out. Half the lights were blown out making the cavernous sheet metal dock as dim as dusk.

The only thing that wasn't cheap on this ship was the nine-by-nineteen-foot wooden crate that towered over me by at least two yards. It was bolted to the floor in the center of the dock to protect it from floating into any walls during shipment. And it was the only thing in the ship.

I didn't know what was on the inside yet but the wood alone would've cost more than the ship. Wood was rare for spacefaring humans. Unless you're living on a newly colonized world with more forests than cities.

But newly colonized worlds wouldn't have the ability to build ships like this and no self-respecting shipyard would build something this poorly. The insulation, heaters, and lights they had on hand in the yards would be designed to last long space voyages and comfortable living conditions.

You'd have to design something from the ground up to make it this crappy.

Plus access to money was never a problem for me so why I wouldn't just buy a nice delivery ship, like I had every other time, baffled me. Unless I wasn't the one who sent this, which invited a whole new mess of problems I wasn't interested in thinking about.

While I was pondering this mystery Gretchen was, quite literally, bouncing off the walls.

None of the mag boots I had fit her. Since I was the only person who was ever supposed to stay on this satellite I hadn't packed any variation in sizes. So Gretchen was enjoying zero-g gymnastics in the wide-open room.

She flipped and twirled in the air as packing material started to litter the room. Soon enough the contents of the container were exposed. Which only added to my confusion about the situation.

Unfortunately, it was not a shipment of liquor or any other drug to alleviate my headache. Although, that dream had evaporated as soon as I stepped on the cheap delivery ship. To make matters worse the device in front of me only added to my headache.

A little over a half dozen pantry-sized server racks with wires, fans, and sheet metal sidings were covered with organs that throbbed and pulsed as if blood pumped through them. The organs themselves were various shades of blue, green, and purple.

As I looked at the device closer I could see that veins branched off of the meaty main organs and connected themselves to the ports and wires of the servers.

I walked around the disgusting behemoth of a machine, my mag-boots clanging on the ground with each step, I noticed the inconsistent thud coming quietly from the room. I thought it was my own heart pulsing in my chest from the excitement I felt about the strange entity in front of me. But all things considered, I felt pretty calm.

"There's a heart in the center of this thing," Gretchen said from above me.

I looked up and she was hanging upside down from the ceiling of the dock, her bare feet hooked around a handhold. Her long blonde ponytail floated behind her. Each individual strand reached out in a unique direction unhindered by gravity.

"It's the size of a kid, deep purple, and hanging between some of these cabinets with some white sinew. What the hell is this?"

"I've never seen anything like it," I replied walking around to the front of the machine, or at least the part closest to the airlock we entered from.

"It's pretty gross," Gretchen said.

I ignored the rest of Gretchen's unhelpful commentary as I noticed a few things that looked passively familiar.

The front of the machine had a chair, well more like an inclined bench you would find at a gym, but it was one of the most familiar things there. Additionally, a CRT TV was embedded into a server rack near the chair with an old keyboard hanging under it. The layout was QWERTY which was familiar to me but not this universe. The keyboard connected to the satellite in the main room was the Freckman layout and covered in dust.

To add to the out-of-time and out-of-universe, nature of this device light-tan masking tape held a USB drive to the TV monitor. USB was going out of style during the life I lived with my Gretchen, why it was taped to this device was beyond me. I didn't even think I had a way to plug this into the satellite's main computer.

Written on the tape in neatly printed orthogonal letters were the words Good Luck.

Gretchen landed next to me as I stared at the strange amalgam of technology in front of me. She linked her arm under my armpit to hold herself to the ground next to me.

"That handwriting," she said.

"I know."

"It looks like Todd's."

I pulled the USB stick off the monitor and the rapid squeaking sound of the tape coming free temporarily rang over the thuds of the beating heart. I balled the tape and tossed it into the air with the rest of the packing material.

"Did you send this to yourself?" Gretchen asked

"Seems like it," I answered. "Thankfully."

"But you don't know what it is?"

"That's the bummer about time travel," I said. "A future version of me must have sent it."

"You know what it reminds me of?" Gretchen asked after a moment of staring at it.

"The floor of a butcher's shop?" I'd started to notice the putrid smell of blood and it brought back an ancient memory of eating salty cabidela in Portugal.

"The Mother Tree. She grew rooms, equipment, doors, and a bunch of other stuff, it was all made out of plants, even really complicated stuff that I hadn't expected to be made out of plants."

"I've never seen a plant with a heart in it."

I turned my back on the machine and headed for the airlock. The monstrosity had lasted who knows how long in space, it could be ignored a few more hours.

Gretchen clung to my arm weightlessly following me to the door. Her first step back into the satellite was a bit wobbly as the artificial gravity field took its effect on her.

"When I asked the avians about why She did that," Gretchen continued as I unstrapped my mag boots, "they said she uses what she knows. Plant matter can carry as much, if not more information than computers if you know how to manipulate it. And She knew how to manipulate it."

I grunted in agreement as I thought about the intricate wooden doors and the simulated apartment I saw on my short visit to the Mother Tree. "We do that eventually. But it doesn't work out." I put my rubber-soled boots on and shoved my laces behind the tongue, too lazy to tie them. I started walking down the long tube-like satellite hallway.

"We as in you and me?" Gretchen asked, her bare feet pitter-pattering on the metal floor behind me.

"We as in humanity. A couple times. It never goes well."

"Maybe this is another attempt at that."

I shook my head. "I hope not. Difference between humanity and the Mother Tree is that, like you said, She knew what She was doing."

"And humanity doesn't?"

"We rarely do," I said with a sigh. "At least not in the beginning. Humanity's like a dog, mindlessly sticking its nose places it doesn't belong. And unlike computers biology can evolve out of our control."

As we entered the central room of the satellite Gretchen headed straight for the seating pit where she'd left her socks and shoes. "Are there any pets you like?"

"I enjoyed beekeeping for a while. But I don't want anything to do with this thing. I have half a mind to jettison that thing into the sun."

Gretchen laughed, and it was nice to hear the satellite filled with a melodious chime that wasn't a computer notification.

"I'm serious. The only thing stopping me is that whatever future version of me sent this would know I burnt this one up and will probably send a second next week."

"You really are your own worst enemy," Gretchen said with a smile as she pulled on her socks. "Ever think it might be a past version of yourself you can't remember."

"I try not to," I said with a groan as I plopped myself into the high-backed chair under the satellite's monitors. I faced away from the screens and looked down at Gretchen seated in the middle of the room.

"My toes are cold, do you have anything warmer than these?" She gestured at the thin neon green and pink athletic socks she wore.

"Not in your size."

"Right now I don't care but I'd like to eventually get that fixed."

With a sigh I rotated my chair and placed the USB stick onto the desk my monitors loomed over. "You're serious?"

"About wanting warm socks? Yes. You were in that ship. It was freezing."

"About staying here."

"Also yes," she said as she walked out of the seating pit, the socks softened her steps. "If you don't mind having me around."

I sat back in my tall armchair and looked up at the ceiling of the satellite. It was smooth metal plates connected to thick metal bracers like the panels of a beach ball. I thought about how much work there was to do, to find my memories, understand my powers, and figure out what the monstrosity that was delivered to me was. An extra set of hands might be worth it.

"If not, like you said, you can drop me off somewhere comfortable and pick me up when you're ready to wipe the tracking memory from me." She stood next to me now, looking down at me as I sat back in my chair.

"And what if I never figure out how to do that?"

"Then I hope you leave me somewhere real nice. I'm thinking somewhere coastal, pre-spacefaring but post-internet. At minimum put me somewhere post indoor plumbing. I'd kill for a hot bath, with some bubbles..."

Gretchen droned on. Her voice was familiar and comforting even if her personality was, at times, grating and contradicted what I was used to.

I took a deep breath and reached out to travel through the multiverse.

"Where are you going?" Gretchen asked placing her hand on my shoulder.

"To get you some changes of clothes," I said as I peeled her hand off. "And to get something to read this USB drive. I'll be back in no time."

"Do you know my size?"

"I was married to you for over a century of combined time."

"You were married to a different version of me," Gretchen clarified. "And this means you're okay with me staying."

"You're right it was a different version of you. But I look forward to getting to know you. And working alongside you."

She wasn't the Gretchen I'd spent a lifetime with, shared countless memories with. But then again I wasn't the nerdy Todd she'd known either. We were both, somehow, the same but different people to each other. And maybe, despite how uncomfortable it'd be at times, that wasn't the worst thing in the world.

"Computer doesn't have any security on it," I added, standing up to give her the seat. "There didn't seem to be a point since I was going to be the only one here. It can give you a tour and show you where the spa is."

"Serious!? There's a spa on board?"

I shrugged with a slight smile. "When I built this I was one of the wealthiest people in the Central System. It was easier to accept the installation of the spa and basketball court."

"You're the only one here, why do you have a basketball court."

I shrugged and took a deep breath to go.

"Thanks, Todd." She gave me an unexpected hug holding down my arms in the process.

I patted her back, unable to free my arms to return the gesture. After what felt like longer than any hug needed to last she let go and took a seat in front of the looming monitors.

"Clothes should be here in an hour or two," I said as I took a deep breath. There were a lot of errands to run, but there was one place I wanted to visit first.

With a focused breath, I hooked onto the universe I wanted to visit.

***

I sat on the uncomfortably flat lid of a porcelain toilet. Humid air surrounded me and clung to my exposed neck and hands. The top half of the room's mirror had started to fog up. The bathroom door had a small gap in it, but it wasn't enough to relieve the room of its humidity.

It was big enough for a streak of orange, startled by my appearance, to disappear out of the room.

Across from my seat on the toilet Gretchen slowly turned her head to face me. She was lying in the bathtub under a mountain of bubbles. Her blonde hair was pulled up into a bun.

She looked me up and down, her eyes bloodshot from sleep deprivation, large purple bags hung at the top of her cheeks.

She looked at me with familiar recognition, but not shock or horror. I'd met her before, but she'd only seen me in dreams so far. She turned her head back to stare up at the shower head mounted high on the wall.

The bathroom counter was covered in plastic makeup cartridges standing like a chaotic crowd at a rock concert. Soon the cat would knock them to the ground.

My long leather jacket hung on my shoulders. I wanted to take it off because of the heat of the room. But leaving it here would alert the past version of me that unwillingly visits of my presence. Plus I was short on time.

So I let the jacket hang heavy on my back. It seemed fitting for my visit.

"Sorry to barge in on you like this."

"Not much you can do to me now," her words were slow but clear. "I beat you to the punch."

"Wish you hadn't," I said solemnly.

Gretchen gave me a dismissive hrmph.

"Your dreams. They really happened. Across the multiverse."

"I had a feeling," Gretchen replied.

"And I'm sorry that I killed you so many times. Across all those realities."

As I took a moment to figure out what to say next Gretchen's phone rang. It sat next to me on the counter, the familiar ringtone was far too chipper for the foggy room.

"You want me to answer that for you?" I asked. Jenna was calling. We both knew why.

"She wouldn't get it."

"Probably not," I agreed. "But it might be worth it to spend time with someone familiar around... here at the end."

"Unfortunately, you're pretty familiar to me."

"You ask me, in a few minutes, if it was worth it? If what I got out of it was worth this misery I'm causing you. I didn't have a chance to answer you. I don't really think I knew the answer then either."

After a moment of silence, Gretchen asked, "And?"

"It wasn't worth it. And I'm sorry for that."

Gretchen laughed from her belly. It was genuine but haunting.

Once the laughter died down to a chuckle she asked, "You couldn't have lied to me?"

I chuckled with her now that I understood the joke. "It's not like I haven't lied to you before. But no. Right now, you deserve the truth. It was selfish and pointless and ruined a lot of lives. Lives I value now. I wish I'd valued them earlier but—"

Gretchen's phone rang again. I shut it off and the tabby cat poked his head in the bathroom.

"It's okay Mr. Porkchops," Gretchen said.

He was rightfully hesitant to walk in further than a few steps.

She tried to lure him in with a few tsking sounds. But he refused to go any further. I couldn't blame him.

"But," I continued, "we figured out how to stop the nightmares. As much as you can stop something that happens simultaneously across time. A version of you gained the power to travel the multiverse like me. Hopefully, she will keep me in check."

"Lucky her."

"Hopefully she won't have to," I added. "I'll do better. For her. For you. For all of you."

"Shouldn't be hard. Just don't go around killing innocent girls." Gretchen's tone was gentle and melodic. It was familiar but I noticed a tiredness in the statement I hadn't heard before.

"I hope it's that straightforward," I replied. The monstrosity sitting in a delivery ship attached to my satellite home, missing memories, and avians that were on the hunt for me made me wonder if anything would ever be straightforward again.

"Try to make things better too." Gretchen rolled her head over to look at me. Her eyebrows were somewhat wrinkled with seriousness. The Gretchen at the Fortress of Solitude would be proud of her for her firmness. "It's the least you can do."

I nodded in agreement and took a deep and focused breath. I had errands to run, clothes to order, and important promises to keep.

There was nothing more I could do for the Gretchen in front of me. But that didn't mean I couldn't make things better for others.

A Roar Through Time – Available Now

Todd Rungson can travel through time and the multiverse with a single breath. He's seen it all, including his death, multiple times.

But that doesn't make being murdered in your sleep any less unnerving.

With an infinite multiverse for the murderer to hid in and no good leads Todd might have met his match.

If you enjoy mind-bending multiverse time travel stories then you'll enjoy the third book of the Endless Breath Saga: A Roar Through Time.

Get A Roar Through Time Today: https://books2read.com/RoarThroughTime

Also By Nicholas Licalsi

The Slugs of Dale Cannon

Rystole Whitlock, a young rancher and colonists on the Earth-like planet of Dale Cannon, spends his days cutting class and herding buffcows.

When a group of alien slugs invade his family's cabin he can't find a good way to corral them before the toxic slugs put his mother in a coma.

Determined to save his mom, and the rest of the colony, Rystole won't stop until he gets revenge or a cure.

If you enjoy exploring alien worlds and first contact stories with young heroes then you'll enjoy Slugs of Dale Cannon.

https://books2read.com/SlugsOfDaleCannon

The Hacked Manticore and Other Cyberpunk Stories

Bett the hacker gets a personalized message on a computer he just broke into. J-Red the streamer accepts a mobster's job offer to get his belongings out of repo. Pairs of packages and pizzas arrive at the doorstep of recently unemployed Kiran.

The cyberpunk world of Galleria Valley runs on corporate greed, shady mob deals, and bionic enhancements. No one survives long when playing by the rules.

Let these short stories be the neon lights that guide your hovercar through the towering buildings of Galleria Valley.
https://books2read.com/HackedManticore

A Trial of Rock and Rope

Upon his death, Ferrun Monteiro wakes up in the afterlife. Instead of building paradise the gods have designed a challenge.

To escape the afterlife Ferrun must reach the top of a mountain with a boulder tied to his ankle.

Yet not a single soul has completed this seemingly simple trial.

Unperturbed, Ferrun faces the god's challenge head on. Follow him on his odyssey through the afterlife.

If you enjoy dreaming about the afterlife, you'll enjoy A Trial of Rock and Rope.

https://books2read.com/ATrialOfRockAndRope

About the Author

Nicholas Licalsi's love for science fiction and fantasy started with a box of his grandfather's pulp paperbacks and the brainwashing alien parasite nesting between their pages. This led to an interest in engineering, robotics, and time travel.

After a successful enough career in software development Nicholas now spends his time trying to trick his overactive imagination into paying the bills while he satiates his dog's need to be pet.

He currently has 9 independently published books available everywhere books are sold and countless short stories on his blog StepInto TheRoad.com. You can get a free book, and updates about his writing, time traveling, and (most importantly) his dog by signing up for his email list at StepIntoTheRoad.com/SignUp

You can connect with me at: https://stepintotheroad.com

Get updates about my upcoming books at: https://stepintoth eroad.com/signup